Harold R Foster

Prince Valiant

COMPRISING PAGES 1729 THROUGH 1772

Knight's Blood

FANTAGRAPHICS BOOKS

ABOUT THIS EDITION:

Produced in cooperation with the Danish publisher Carlsen and several other publishers around the world, this new edition of PRINCE VALIANT is intended to be the definitive compilation of Hal Foster's masterpiece.

In addition to this volume, Fantagraphics Books has in stock thirty-two more collections of Foster's Prince Valiant work (Vols. 1-2 and 9-38). The ultimate goal is to have the entirety of Hal Foster's epic, comprising 40 volumes, in print at once.

ABOUT THE PUBLISHER:

FANTAGRAPHICS BOOKS has dedicated itself to bringing readers the finest in comic book and comic strip material, both new and old. Its "classics" division includes *The Complete E.C. Segar Popeye*, the *Complete Little Nemo in Slumberland* hardcover collection, and *Pogo* and *Little Orphan Annie* reprints. Its "modern" division is responsible for such works as *Love and Rockets* by Los Bros. Hernandez, Peter Bagge's *Hate*, Daniel Clowes's *Eightball*, Chris Ware's *ACME*, and American editions of work by Muñoz & Sampayo, Lewis Trondheim, and F. Solano Lopez, as well as *The Complete Crumb Comics*.

PREVIOUS VOLUMES IN THIS SERIES:

PRINCE VALIANT, Volume 39
"Knight's Blood"
comprising pages 1729 (March 29, 1970) through 1772 (January 24, 1971)
Published by Fantagraphics Books, 7563 Lake City Way NE, Seattle, WA 98115
Editorial Co-Ordinator: Henning Kure and Jens Trasborg
Colored by Jesper Ejsing
Cover inked by Jan Kjær
Fantagraphics Books staff: Kim Thompson and Carrie Whitney
Copyright © 2000 King Features Syndicate, Inc., Bull's, Interpresse, & Fantagraphics Books, Inc.
Printed in Denmark
ISBN 1-56097-388-9
First Printing: Spring, 2000

Prince Valiant
IN THE DAYS OF KING ARTHUR
BY HAROLD R FOSTER

Our Story: PRINCE VALIANT FOLLOWS THE DEER TRACKS RIGHT TO THE EDGE OF THE THICKET. IT IS PLAIN THAT THEY HAVE BEEN DRIVEN OUT OF THE KING'S FOREST. "ALL RIGHT, HUGH-THE-FOX, COME ON OUT AND EXPLAIN!" SHOUTS VAL.

"WELL, IF IT ISN'T SIR VALIANT OF PLEASANT MEMORY! WHY ARE YOU SHATTERING OUR WOODLAND QUIET WITH YOUR BELLOWING?" ASKS HUGH, STEPPING INTO THE OPEN.

"BY THE TRACKS, I SUSPECT YOU AND YOUR BAND OF THIEVING RASCALS HAVE DRIVEN ALL THE DEER FROM THE KING'S FOREST, AND THE KING IS WRATH.".
"TUT, TUT," ANSWERS HUGH, "HIS BAD TEMPER WILL SPOIL HIS APPETITE. TAKE ME TO HIM."

VAL INTRODUCES HIS COMPANION: "SIRE, THIS IS HUGH-THE-FOX, FORMER LEADER OF OUTLAWS WHOM YOU PARDONED AFTER HE AND HIS BAND SERVED YOU AS SCOUTS AND LED YOUR KNIGHTS THROUGH THE FORESTS OF KENT TO SURPRISE AND DEFEAT A SAXON ARMY. HE KNOWS WHERE YOUR DEER HAVE GONE."

ARTHUR IS ANGRY: "YOU KNOW THE PENALTY FOR TAKING DEER IN THE KING'S FOREST, DO YOU NOT?"
"YES, SIRE," ANSWERS HUGH WITH A GRIN, "AND NOW YOU KNOW WHAT IT IS LIKE FOR A HUNTER TO GO EMPTY-HANDED."

"YOU RASCAL, ARE YOU TRYING TO BLACKMAIL YOUR KING?" ROARS ARTHUR.
"YES, SIRE!" HUGH RETURNS ANGRILY, "YOU GAVE US PARDON BUT FORBADE US TO HUNT THE DEER. WE LIVE IN THE DEEP WOODS AND MUST HAVE MEAT!"

"SEIZE HIM!" THE KING COMMANDS. "WE ACCUSE HIM OF DISOBEYING THE LAW OF THE LAND."

VAL STEPS FORWARD. "IF HUGH IS TO BE TRIED, THE LAW PERMITS HIM LEGAL ADVICE. I WILL BE HIS ADVOCATE."
NEXT WEEK- Prince Valiant, Lawyer

HAL FOSTER

1729   3-29

Prince Valiant

IN THE DAYS OF KING ARTHUR

BY HAROLD R. FOSTER

Our Story: KING ARTHUR RETURNS TO THE LODGE AFTER A FRUITLESS DAY OF HUNTING. HE IS IN A RAGE, FOR HUGH-THE-FOX AND HIS FORESTERS HAD DRIVEN THE DEER HERD DEEP INTO THE THICKET.

AND HUGH, IN CHAINS, WONDERS IF HIS IMPUDENCE HAS GONE TOO FAR. HE PLACES HIS HOPE IN PRINCE VALIANT. IF ANYONE CAN SOOTHE THE KING, IT IS HE.

AND VAL RIDES ALL NIGHT TO CAMELOT, THERE TO SEARCH THE ARCHIVES FOR A PARDON SIGNED BY ARTHUR SOME FIFTEEN YEARS AGO.

SIR KAY IS PROSECUTOR, A JUST MAN BUT SEVERE. HE BELIEVES IN THE LETTER OF THE LAW; "THE PENALTY IS CLEARLY WRITTEN AND MUST BE ENFORCED. THOUGH IT IS NOT PROVEN THAT HE KILLED ANY, YET HE DROVE AWAY THE WHOLE HERD!"

"LET ME READ FROM THIS DOCUMENT," PLEADS VAL. "'IN GRATITUDE FOR GREAT SERVICES RENDERED TO KING AND COUNTRY, WE GRANT FULL PARDON TO HUGH-THE-FOX AND HIS BAND OF OUTLAWS AND GIVE THEM THE FREEDOM OF OUR FORESTS. SIGNED: ARTHUR, REX!'"

"LET US HEAR FROM HUGH," THE KING COMMANDS. "SIRE, WE HAVE OBEYED YOUR LAWS, WE HAVE TRAINED YOUNG MEN AS SCOUTS TO SERVE YOU IN WAR, BUT WE WERE BETTER OFF AS OUTLAWS. WE ARE FORESTERS, NOT TILLERS OF THE SOIL. WE LIVE ON NUTS, RABBITS AND BERRIES IN WOODLANDS TEEMING WITH DEER. MANY OF MY BAND HAVE RETURNED TO THEIR OLD OUTLAW WAYS."

1730

© King Features Syndicate, Inc., 1970. World rights reserved.

4-5

"OUTLAWS AND POACHERS CAN EXPECT THE HANGMAN'S NOOSE," INTERRUPTS SIR KAY. "SO WHAT?" SHOUTS HUGH ANGRILY. "OUR LOYALTY TO THE KING AND HIS LAWS IS REWARDED WITH STARVATION!"

NEXT WEEK — Temper! Temper!

HAL FOSTER

1730

Prince Valiant

IN THE DAYS OF KING ARTHUR

BY HAROLD R FOSTER

Our Story RELATES OF HOW HUGH-THE-FOX RISKED THE HANGMAN'S NOOSE BY DRIVING ALL THE DEER OUT OF THE KING'S PARK IN ORDER TO CALL THE KING'S ATTENTION TO THE PLIGHT OF THE FOREST PEOPLE.

"YOU KNOW FULL WELL WE MUST HARVEST THE DEER TO FEED THE PEOPLE OF CAMELOT THROUGH THE WINTER, YET YOU SPOILED OUR HUNT."

"THE DEER ARE BACK ERE NOW, MY LIEGE. HARVEST THEM IN GREAT NUMBERS THOUGH THEY BE LEAN AND SCRAWNY. FOR WHEN SPRING COMES ALL THAT ARE LEFT WILL BE DEAD FROM STARVATION," ANSWERS HUGH. "MY GAMEKEEPERS PROMISED ME ABUNDANT VENISON THIS SEASON. DID THEY NOT KEEP THEIR PROMISE?" ASKS ARTHUR.

"ALL TOO WELL!" HUGH REPLIES. "TO WIN YOUR PRAISE THEY NOT ONLY INCREASED THE HERD BUT DROVE IN MORE DEER FROM OTHER FORESTS. EVEN THE MOST IGNORANT PEASANT DOES NOT PUT MORE SHEEP IN A PASTURE THAN THAT PASTURE CAN SUPPORT. NOW YOUR PARK IS BROWSED CLEAN, EVEN THE BARK IS NIBBLED FROM THE TREES."

"AND WHAT WOULD YOU ADVISE?" THE KING INQUIRES, FORGETTING THAT ONLY A MOMENT AGO HE WAS READY TO STRETCH HUGH'S IMPUDENT NECK. "PERHAPS YOU MIGHT BE WILLING TO TEACH MY GAMEKEEPERS HOW TO MANAGE THE HERD?"

"NO, SIRE, YOUR MEN ARE TOO STUPID AND TOO PROUD TO ACCEPT MY AUTHORITY. IT WOULD BE USELESS." "AS HUGH'S ADVOCATE, MAY I OFFER A SUGGESTION?" ASKS VAL.

"WHY TRY TO TRAIN MEN ALREADY PROVEN INCOMPETENT WHEN HUGH AND HIS BAND ARE THE BEST FORESTERS IN THE LAND? PERHAPS FOR THE PRIVILEGE OF HUNTING THEY MIGHT AGREE TO BECOME WARDENS OF THE KING'S FORESTS."

ARTHUR GLARES AT VAL: "THIS IS WHAT YOU HAD IN MIND WHEN YOU BROUGHT THIS IMPUDENT RASCAL HERE, WAS IT NOT? REQUEST GRANTED. AND TAKE THAT GRIN OFF YOUR FACE!"

NEXT WEEK — The Hunt

HAL FOSTER

Prince Valiant
IN THE DAYS OF KING ARTHUR
BY HAROLD R. FOSTER

Our Story: A GREAT AMOUNT OF VENISON MUST BE STORED FOR THE WINTER MONTHS, A HUGE UNDERTAKING. BUT ARTHUR GOT THE HELP OF KNIGHT AND NOBLE BY TURNING THE HUNT INTO A SPORTING EVENT. THE YOUNG BRITONS' LOVE OF DANGER ADDED MANY INNOVATIONS; WHEN THE HOUNDS BROUGHT A STAG TO BAY ONE WOULD BRAVE HORNS AND HOOVES TO BRING IT DOWN ARMED ONLY WITH KNIFE OR SPEAR.

WHEN THE BUTCHERS' CARTS RUMBLE BACK TO THE CASTLE THEY OFTEN BRING A TOO VENTURESOME OR TOO CLUMSY KNIGHT ALONG WITH OTHER RESULTS OF THE HUNT.

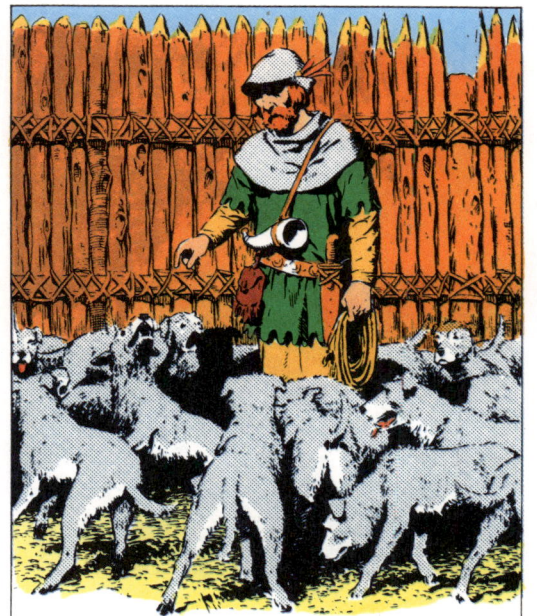

AT DAY'S END THE HUNTERS MAKE MERRY AT A HUNT BANQUET, BUT THERE IS NO JOY IN THE HEART OF THE MASTER OF HOUNDS. HE COUNTS HIS BELOVED COMPANIONS.

THEN TAKES UP A SPADE AND GOES BACK OVER THE HUNTING GROUNDS AND DOES WHAT MUST BE DONE. HE HOLDS BACK THE TEARS BY REPEATING: "IT'S ONLY A DOG, ONLY A DOG."

SOON WINTER WILL PUT AN END TO GAIETY AND EVERYONE WILL RETIRE TO THEIR SNUG HOMES. MEANWHILE THESE LAST DAYS OF AUTUMN ARE TO BE ENJOYED TO THE FULLEST, WITH ENOUGH ROMANCE TO GOSSIP ABOUT UNTIL SPRING.

THE YOUNG KNIGHTS FIGHT LIKE LIONS IN THE TOURNAMENTS, FOR ONLY THE BRAVEST AND BEST ARE PRIVILEGED TO MEET THE CHAMPIONS OF THE ROUND TABLE, A GREAT HONOR.

AMONG THE MANY YOUNG WARRIORS WHO HAVE COME TO CAMELOT TO WIN THE GOLDEN SPURS OF KNIGHTHOOD IS DALE MAKINNIE...... BUT WHY CONTINUE, WE WILL SEE MORE OF HIM ANON.

NEXT WEEK - The Lady in Domni

HAL FOSTER

1732

4-19

Prince Valiant
IN THE DAYS OF KING ARTHUR
BY HAROLD R. FOSTER

Our Story: THE HARVEST HAS BEEN GATHERED, THE WARS ARE AT AN END, SOON WINTER WILL PUT AN END TO TRAVEL. IN THE MEANWHILE THE COURT MAKES MERRY WITH ALL MANNER OF ENTERTAINMENT. INTO THIS GAY SCENE COMES YOUNG DALE MAKINNIE SEEKING FAME AND FORTUNE.

HE IS DAZZLED BY THE SPLENDOR OF CAMELOT... AND ITS PEOPLE! FAIR LADIES SPARKLING WITH JEWELS AND FAMOUS KNIGHTS WHOSE DEEDS HAVE BECOME LEGENDS STROLL ABOUT OR WATCH THE MANY ENTERTAINERS.

AS AN UNTRIED KNIGHT IN COUNTRY CLOTHES DALE IS AN OUTSIDER. BUT HE VOWS THAT HE WILL SEEK EVERY OPPORTUNITY TO PROVE HIS VALOR AND BECOME ONE OF THESE HEROES.

THE FAME OF THE ROUND TABLE HAS SPREAD THROUGHOUT THE KNOWN WORLD AND MANY WARRIORS FROM DISTANT LANDS COME HITHER SEARCHING FOR ADVENTURE. AND THEY BRING WITH THEM A ROMANTIC IDEAL: THE WORSHIP OF WOMAN AS A SYMBOL OF PURE LOVE. THE 'AGE OF CHIVALRY' IS BORN.

THE IDEA APPEALS TO DALE, TO WORSHIP FROM AFAR A BEAUTIFUL LADY, GRACIOUS, VIRTUOUS AND UNATTAINABLE. TO DO GREAT DEEDS IN HER HONOR, TO BE HER CHAMPION, EVEN DIE IN HER SERVICE!

FIRST HE MUST PROVE HIMSELF WORTHY, SO HE ENTERS THE LISTS AND CONTENDS WITH SUCH RECKLESS DETERMINATION THAT HE WINS THE RIGHT TO CHALLENGE ONE OF THE KNIGHTS OF THE ROUND TABLE.

WITH THE PURSE HE WON HE BUYS RAIMENT SUITABLE TO A CHAMPION-TO-BE. WHOM SHALL HE CHALLENGE? SIR GAWAIN, THE IRON KNIGHT; BALEN, THE STRONG; SIR VALIANT, THE NIMBLE; OR EVEN THE MIGHTY LAUNCELOT HIMSELF?

1733 © King Features Syndicate, Inc., 1970. World rights reserved. 4-26

SUCH IS THE OVERCONFIDENCE OF YOUTH THAT HE WONDERS IF THERE IS A LADY WORTHY OF HIS DEVOTION. THEN HE SEES ALETA!

NEXT WEEK— **Romance and Bruises**

HAL FOSTER

Prince Valiant

IN THE DAYS OF KING ARTHUR

BY HAROLD R FOSTER

Our Story: DALE MAKINNIE SEARCHES CAMELOT TO FIND A LADY FAIR WORTHY TO BE HIS LADY-IN-DOMNI. ONE TO LOVE FROM A DISTANCE AND INSPIRE HIM TO PERFORM MIGHTY DEEDS. THEN ALETA WALKS BY.

TO BE A KNIGHT IN HER SERVICE HE WOULD CONQUER THE WORLD. AS A BEGINNING THERE IS THE CHALLENGE ROUND WHERE TOURNAMENT WINNERS CAN TRY THEIR PROWESS AGAINST KNIGHTS OF THE ROUND TABLE.

HE PICKS ONE OF THE MOST RENOWNED: SIR GAWAIN. GAWAIN IS NOT IN THE BEST CONDITION, HAVING SPENT THE NIGHT AT THE GAMING TABLE, AND IS ANXIOUS TO RETURN TO THE DICE.

ON THE FIRST COURSE GAWAIN MISSES THE TARGET AND WOULD HAVE BEEN DISMOUNTED HAD NOT DALE'S LANCE SHATTERED. GAWAIN'S PRIDE IS HURT AND SO IS EVERY BONE IN HIS BODY. ON THE NEXT CHARGE HE PLUCKS THE YOUNG UPSTART FROM HIS SADDLE.

AS DALE IS HELPED FROM THE LISTS HE IS AWARE THAT THE KNIGHTS OF THE ROUND TABLE ARE NOT AS ORDINARY MEN AND HE HAS A LONG WAY TO GO BEFORE HE CAN EARN A PLACE AMONG THEM.

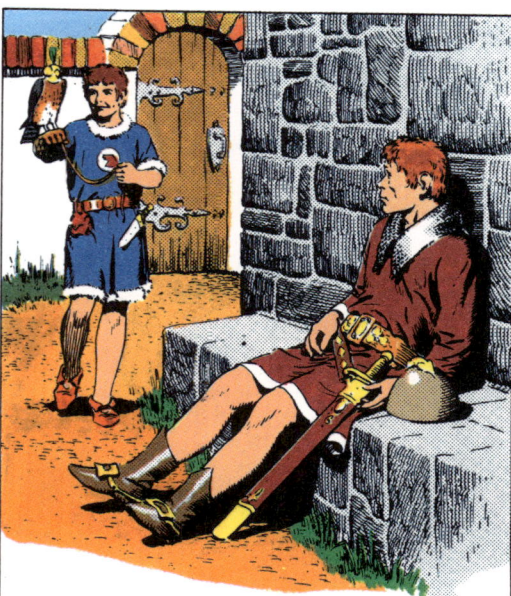

AS HE SITS BRUISED AND DEJECTED, A YOUNG LAD WITH A FALCON ON HIS FIST AND A CHEERFUL GRIN ON HIS FACE STROLLS UP. "YOU SHOOK UP SIR GAWAIN. HE IS IN HIS PAVILION NOW GROWLING LIKE A WOUNDED BEAR."

A MUTUAL LOVE OF HAWKING LEADS TO FRIENDSHIP, AND DALE IS INVITED TO DINNER.

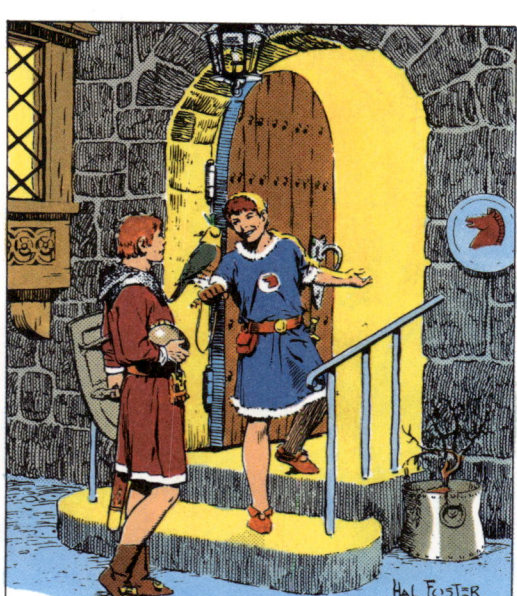

AND HE ENTERS THE HOUSE IN SOME EMBARRASSMENT, FOR HE HAS FAILED TO FIND OUT HIS HOST'S NAME.

NEXT WEEK – The Unattainable Lady

HAL FOSTER

1734

© King Features Syndicate, Inc., 1970. World rights reserved.

5-3

Prince Valiant

IN THE DAYS OF KING ARTHUR

BY HAROLD R FOSTER

Our Story: PRINCE ARN INVITES HIS NEW-FOUND FRIEND TO HIS HOME. AND DALE MAKINNIE IS EMBARRASSED, FOR HE DOES NOT YET KNOW HIS HOST'S NAME.

THEN HE SEES HER, HIS IDEAL, THE LADY UNATTAINABLE, IN WHOSE HONOR HE WOULD DO GREAT DEEDS. TO WORSHIP HER AT A DISTANCE IS ONE THING, BUT TO SEE HER SO CLOSE IS OVERWHELMING. DIMLY HE HEARS HIS HOST SAY, "MOTHER, THIS IS DALE MAKINNIE, WHO JOUSTED WITH GAWAIN TODAY. DALE, THIS IS MY MOTHER, QUEEN ALETA OF THE MISTY ISLES."

AS HE KISSES HER SMALL, FIRM HAND HE MUMBLES SOMETHING. HE KNOWS HE IS ACTING LIKE A CLUMSY STABLEBOY BUT CAN'T HELP IT.

SHE SOON PUTS HIM AT EASE AND GETS HIM TO TALK OF HIS HOME AND AMBITIONS. EVEN WHEN SHE PICKS UP A WOODEN SPOON AND RAPS GALAN'S KNUCKLES SHE MAKES IT A QUEENLY GESTURE.

"ACCURSED LUCK! MARRIED, MOTHER OF A FAMILY AND TWICE MY AGE. CAN I WORSHIP HER FROM AFAR AS MY LADY-IN-DOMNI OR WILL I BECOME HER FAWNING PUPPY-DOG?"

OTHER KNIGHTS SPEAK OF CHIVALRY IN HIGH-SOUNDING TERMS: WOMAN ON A PEDESTAL, IMAGINATION ENDOWING HER WITH EVERY VIRTUE, AN IDEAL. THERE IS A FAIRY-TALE QUALITY TO THIS CONCEPT THAT PUZZLES DALE.

FOR HIS CHOSEN LADY IS ALL TOO REAL. HE HAS HEARD HER SOFT AEGEAN ACCENT, HER READY LAUGH. HOW CAN HE WORSHIP FROM AFAR ONE SO GRACIOUS AND FRIENDLY? IS HE BECOMING INFATUATED, AND WILL HE MAKE AN ASS OF HIMSELF?

NEXT WEEK— **Yes, Dale**

5-10

© King Features Syndicate, Inc. 1970. World rights reserved.

1735

Prince Valiant IN THE DAYS OF KING ARTHUR
BY HAROLD R. FOSTER

Our Story: DALE MAKINNIE HAS SPENT A SLEEPLESS NIGHT, WONDERING IF HE IS STRONG ENOUGH TO CONCEAL HIS INFATUATION FOR QUEEN ALETA AND SO AVOID EMBARRASSMENT. THEN ARN INVITES HIM TO GO A-HAWKING.

IN THE MEWS THEY CHOOSE THEIR FALCONS. HOODED AND JESSED, THE BIRDS ARE CALM, BUT THE NERVOUS RUFFLING OF FEATHERS SHOWS THEY KNOW THAT SOON THEY WILL ONCE MORE ROAM THE SKY.

BEFORE THE DAY ENDS A FIRM FRIENDSHIP IS FORMED.

WHILE THEY ARE HAVING REFRESHMENTS ALETA WALKS IN. ONE GLANCE AT DALE'S ADORING EYES AND SHE KNOWS FROM LONG EXPERIENCE THAT SHE HAS TROUBLED ANOTHER YOUNG HEART. AND THE CURE FOR THAT IS TO FIND HIM A SUITABLE MAID HIS OWN AGE.

THE TWINS ARE WHOLE-HEARTEDLY IN FAVOR OF THE NEW CULT OF CHIVALRY, AND VALETA IS ALREADY DEEPLY IN LOVE WITH A YOUNG GOTHIC KNIGHT. KAREN FIXES A STERN GAZE ON DALE. SHE EYES HIM FROM HEAD TO TOE AS ONE MIGHT A HORSE OFFERED FOR SALE.

"THIS SCARF WILL BE CARRIED INTO BATTLE BY SOME YOUNG KNIGHT AS MY FAVOR TO INSPIRE HIM TO DO NOBLE DEEDS. I HAVE NOT YET CHOSEN THE KNIGHT."

"OF COURSE MOTHER IS TOO OLD FOR ROMANCE. BESIDES, IT WOULD SEEM THAT EVERY KNIGHT IN CAMELOT HAS BEGGED TO CARRY HER TALISMAN UNTIL SHE IS COMPLETELY WITHOUT SCARVES AND KERCHIEFS."

1736 © King Features Syndicate, Inc., 1970. World rights reserved. 5-17

WHEN KAREN HAS LEFT, ARN REMARKS: "YOU KNOW MUCH ABOUT HORSES AND HAWKS. NOW YOU WILL LEARN SOMETHING ABOUT WOMEN."

NEXT WEEK—**Ah! Women!**

Prince Valiant
IN THE DAYS OF KING ARTHUR
BY Harold R Foster

Our Story: CHIVALRY, THE AGE OF ROMANCE, ENVELOPS CAMELOT LIKE AN EPIDEMIC. KING ARTHUR FINDS THIS NEW IDEAL USEFUL. YOUNG KNIGHTS ARE WILLING TO ACCEPT EVEN THE DULLEST QUESTS IN ORDER TO BRING HONOR TO THEIR LADIES.

THE LADIES FIND IT PLEASANT TO BE SO WORSHIPED EVEN THOUGH THEY MUST LISTEN TO MUCH BAD POETRY IN PRAISE OF THEIR EYES, THEIR GRACE AND OTHER ASSORTED CHARMS.

SLEEP TOO IS INTERRUPTED BY FORLORN GALLANTS WHO SING OF UNDYING LOVE FOR THEIR FAIR LADIES, VIRTUOUS AND UNATTAINABLE. BALLADS THAT SEEM ENDLESS AND NOT ALWAYS IN KEY.

THE ADORED ONES TRY HARD TO BELIEVE IN THESE FLATTERIES. HUSBANDS, ON THE OTHER HAND, TAKE A DIM VIEW OF ALL THIS ROMANTIC NONSENSE.

IMPETUOUS YOUTH MAY FOLLOW THE WILL-O'-WISP OF ROMANCE JUST SO FAR BUT, IN LATER YEARS, FIND IT MORE COMFORTABLE TO SETTLE DOWN, NOT WITH THE IDEAL LADY, BUT SOME COMPETENT WIFE WHO HAD PLANNED TO GET HIM ALL ALONG.

HER TWELFTH BIRTHDAY HAS PASSED AND KAREN HAS PUT AWAY HER PLAYTHINGS AND IS READY FOR ROMANCE. SHE HAS DECIDED TO BECOME DALE'S UNATTAINABLE LADY FAIR, AND PURSUES HIM LIKE A HUNTRESS.

TO MAKE MATTERS WORSE ALETA, TO CURE HIS INFATUATION FOR HER, IS TRYING TO INTEREST HIM IN A MAID HIS OWN AGE.

1737   © King Features Syndicate, Inc., 1970. World rights reserved.   5-24

AND YET ANOTHER FEMALE IS ABOUT TO ENTER DALE'S LIFE. LADY MARVYN IS PLEADING WITH THE KING TO REDRESS A GREAT WRONG.

NEXT WEEK— *The Talisman*

Prince Valiant

IN THE DAYS OF KING ARTHUR

BY Harold R Foster

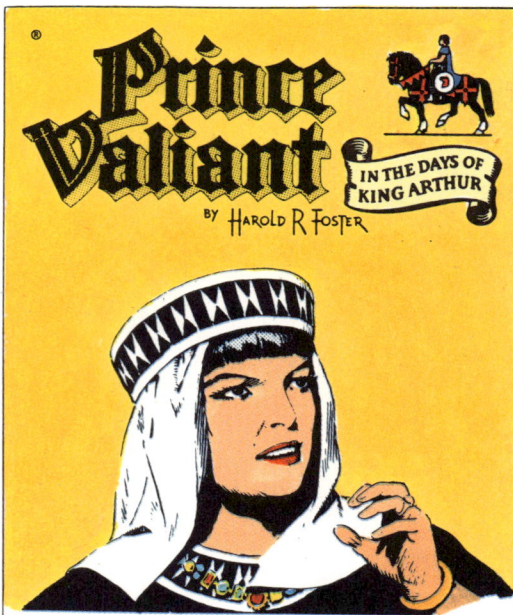

Our Story: THE LADY MARVYN APPEALS TO KING ARTHUR TO REDRESS A GREAT WRONG. AN INHERITANCE IS IN DISPUTE AND FALSE CLAIMANTS ARE TRYING TO OUST HER AND HER SON, THE REAL HEIR.

A HUNDRED ARDENT YOUNG KNIGHTS WILL BE QUARTERED IN CAMELOT OVER THE WINTER, AND IDLENESS WILL BRING TROUBLE. WORK MUST BE FOUND FOR THEM, AND THE KING CALLS THE COUNCIL TOGETHER AND EXPLAINS LADY MARVYN'S PLEA. "WHOM SHALL WE SEND?" HE ASKS. PRINCE VALIANT SPEAKS: "MAY I SUGGEST DALE MAKINNIE, A FINE YOUNG MAN WHO NEEDS THE EXPERIENCE."

DALE IS OVERJOYED. THE MISSION WILL BE A WELCOME RELIEF FROM HIS EMOTIONAL PROBLEMS. VAL TAKES HIM HOME FOR INSTRUCTION, FOR WHO WOULD KNOW MORE ABOUT INHERITANCE LAWS THAN A QUEEN AND A PRINCE?

LADY MARVYN TELLS HER SAD TALE. UPON HER HUSBAND'S DEATH SHE BECAME REGENT OF THE FIEF UNTIL HER SON SHOULD COME OF AGE. THEN HER HUSBAND'S EVIL BROTHER MOVED IN, CLAIMING THE ESTATE AS HIS. FEARING HE MIGHT MURDER HER SON, SHE SENT THE BOY TO A MONASTERY FOR SAFETY.

KAREN MAKES ONE LAST EFFORT. "ARE YOU GOING TO BE MY KNIGHT CHAMPION?" SHE DEMANDS IN HER STRAIGHTFORWARD WAY. "NO," ANSWERS DALE. SHE LOOKS AT HIM ADMIRINGLY. AN HONEST QUESTION DESERVES AN HONEST ANSWER.

SHOULD AN UNTRIED KNIGHT PRESUME TO ASK A QUEEN FOR A TOKEN? ALETA HANDS HIM HER KERCHIEF: "I WOULD BE PLEASED IF YOU CARRIED THIS TO REMIND YOU THAT SHEER COURAGE IS NOT ENOUGH."

1738   © King Features Syndicate, Inc., 1970. World rights reserved.   5-31

SO DALE MAKINNIE RIDES OUT ON HIS FIRST QUEST, A SCENTED TOKEN TUCKED IN HIS BREAST AND A RIDDLE TO SOLVE. WHAT DID SHE MEAN, 'COURAGE IS NOT ENOUGH'?

NEXT WEEK — Enter Sir Lowary

HAL FOSTER

Prince Valiant
IN THE DAYS OF KING ARTHUR
BY HAROLD R. FOSTER

Our Story: IT HAS BEEN RECORDED THAT ALETA IS PASSING FAIR. SHE HAS THE APPROPRIATE NUMBER OF FEATURES NEATLY ARRANGED, AND SUCH LIMBS AND CURVES AS SHE POSSESSES ARE DECORATIVE, BUT THE FARTHER DALE RIDES THE MORE BEAUTIFUL SHE SEEMS.

HE PAYS LITTLE ATTENTION TO LADY MARVYN. SHE TOO IS BEAUTIFUL, BUT SHE TALKS INCESSANTLY OF HER WRONGS, AND THE INNER HATRED MARS THAT BEAUTY.

THEY HALT FOR THE NIGHT AT A POSTHOUSE, AND OVER THE EVENING MEAL DALE BECOMES AWARE THAT SHE IS MORE INTERESTED IN HAVING HER BROTHER-IN-LAW KILLED THAN IN THE LEGAL PROBLEMS.

FROM A HILLTOP MARVYN CASTLE FROWNS DOWN ON A VILLAGE GRAY WITH POVERTY. "YOU RIDE ON WITH YOUR SERVANTS," SUGGESTS DALE. "I WILL STOP HERE AND HAVE MY HARNESS REPAIRED."

SOME NOBLES REGARD CHURL AND SERF AS HARDLY HUMAN AND MAKE NO EFFORT TO CONCEAL ANYTHING FROM THEM. AT THE EXPENSE OF A FEW MUGS OF ALE DALE LEARNS MUCH ABOUT THE STRANGE PEOPLE OF THE CASTLE. IT IS NOT GOOD.

WHEN DALE ENTERS THE CASTLE THE FIRST TO GREET HIM IS TALL SIR LOWARY. IF HE IS INDEED THE VILLAIN OF THE PIECE, HIS EVIL LOOKS CONFIRM IT.

THE EVENING MEAL IS NOT A PLEASANT ONE. "SIR DALE MAKINNIE HAS BEEN SENT BY THE KING TO OUST YOU FROM MY RIGHTFUL HOME," SAYS LADY MARVYN. "NOT SO," SNEERS LOWARY, "ELSE HE WOULD HAVE SENT A MORE FORMIDABLE KNIGHT AND NOT A BEARDLESS BOY." "SHALL WE EXAMINE THE PROOFS ON THE MORROW?" ASKS DALE CALMLY.

NEXT WEEK— Courage is Not Enough

1739 © King Features Syndicate, Inc., 1970. World rights reserved. 6-7

Prince Valiant

IN THE DAYS OF KING ARTHUR

BY HAROLD R. FOSTER

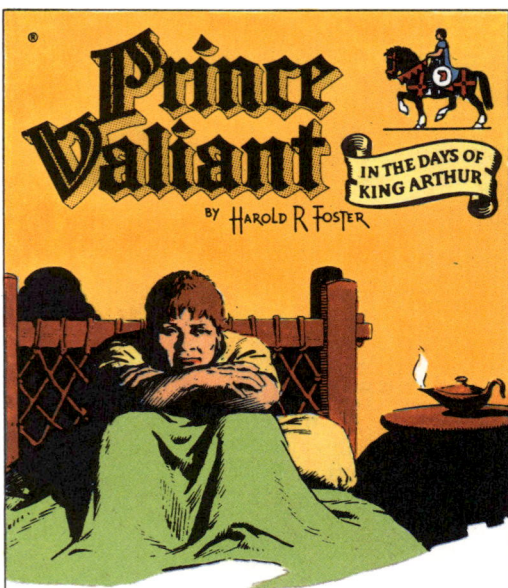

Our Story: DALE SPENDS A SLEEPLESS NIGHT. THE TASK KING ARTHUR HAS ASSIGNED HIM SEEMED SIMPLE: ON THE DEATH OF LORD MARVYN, HIS SON SHOULD INHERIT THE FIEF. BUT WHERE IS THAT SON? THE SERFS IN THE VILLAGE HAVE HINTED THAT HE IS DEAD!

IF THIS IS SO, THEN SIR LOWARY, THE LORD'S BROTHER, IS NEXT IN LINE. THEN WHY ALL THE MYSTERY? PRODUCE THE BOY AND THE CASE IS SETTLED!

ALETA'S FAVOR; STRANGE THAT SUCH A DAINTY TRIFLE COULD REPRESENT ALL THAT IS FINE AND GALLANT. BUT WHAT DID SHE MEAN WHEN SHE SAID, "COURAGE IS NOT ENOUGH"?

THE DAY BEGINS WITH CAUSTIC REMARKS FROM LADY MARVYN. TURNING TO DALE SHE SAYS, "YOU WERE SENT HERE BY THE KING TO DRIVE THIS INTERLOPER FROM MY HOME. DO IT!"
"YES, WHY DON'T YOU?" REMARKS LOWARY WITH A SARDONIC GRIN. BY A GREAT EFFORT DALE CONTROLS HIS ANGER. "WE WILL EXAMINE THE RECORDS FIRST."

A MAN-AT-ARMS ENTERS BEARING LOWARY'S ARMS AND WHISPERS A MESSAGE. AS HE ARMS, DALE SAYS: "BY THE AUTHORITY VESTED IN ME BY THE KING I DEMAND YOU PRODUCE THE RECORDS."
"NEITHER YOU NOR THE KING GIVES ORDERS HERE, SO BE PATIENT, LITTLE MAN, BE PATIENT." EXIT SIR LOWARY, LAUGHING.

"WHERE ARE THE RECORDS?" HE ASKS HER LADYSHIP.
"IN LOWARY'S STRONGBOX, AND HE HAS THE KEYS," SHE REPLIES.

FOR THE FIRST TIME IN HIS LIFE DALE KNOWS HATE. HOW LONG CAN HE SUFFER INSULTS IN ORDER TO COMPLETE THE KING'S MISSION? THEN HE REMEMBERS ALETA'S WORDS: "COURAGE IS NOT ENOUGH."

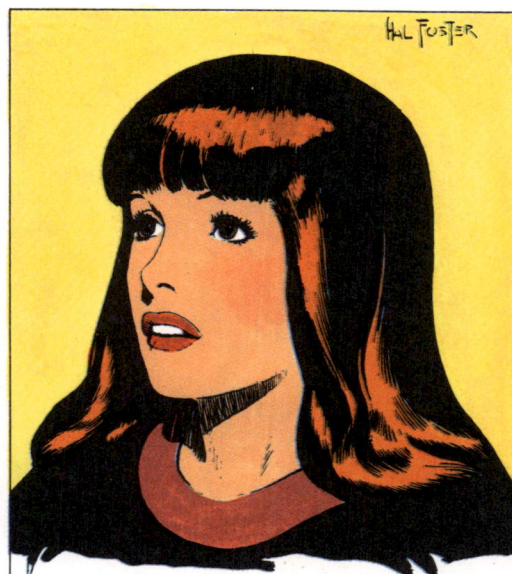

THE FOURTH MEMBER AT THE TABLE RISES. DALE SUPPOSED HER TO BE LADY MARVYN'S MAID, FOR SHE SAT IN SILENCE WITH BOWED HEAD. "YOU DID WELL TO HOLD YOUR TEMPER," SHE SAYS, "BUT THERE IS WORSE TO COME."

NEXT WEEK— The Stepchild

HAL FOSTER

1740   © King Features Syndicate, Inc., 1970. World rights reserved.   6-14

Prince Valiant
IN THE DAYS OF KING ARTHUR
BY HAROLD R FOSTER

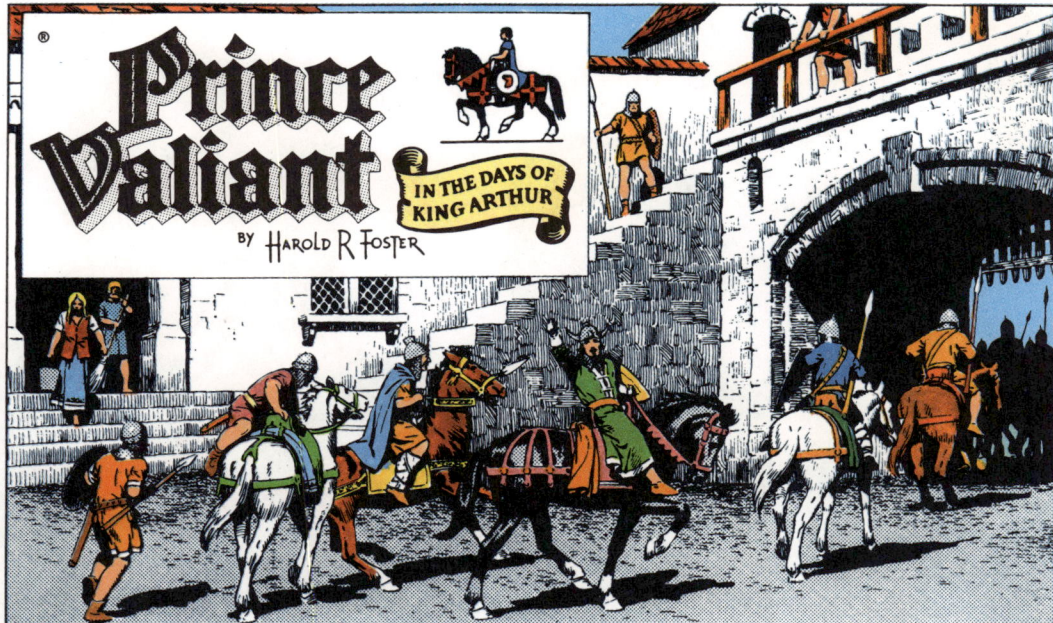

Our Story: A WHISPERED MESSAGE. THEREAFTER SIR LOWARY ARMS HIMSELF AND LEADS A TROOP OF MEN-AT-ARMS CLATTERING FROM THE COURTYARD HEADING WESTWARD TOWARD THE KING'S HIGHWAY, TEN MILES AWAY. AND DALE, TREMBLING WITH RAGE, WATCHES HIM GO AND WONDERS HOW LONG HE CAN BEAR UP UNDER HIS INSULTS.

THE MAID APPROACHES, QUIET AS A SHADOW. "LEAVE THIS HATEFUL PLACE. IT IS NOT WORTH SAVING, AND SIR LOWARY PLANS TO KILL YOU. HIS INSULTS ARE FOR A PURPOSE."

"WHEN YOUR PATIENCE WEARS THIN OR YOUR HONOR IS QUESTIONED YOU WILL HAVE TO CHALLENGE HIM TO A DUEL. IF YOURS IS THE CHALLENGE, HIS WILL BE THE CHOICE OF WEAPONS. HE WILL CHOOSE THE WHIPMACE, WITH WHICH HE IS EXPERT. NEVER HAS HE LOST."

"I AM LORD MARVYN'S DAUGHTER BY HIS FIRST WIFE. THE PRESENT LADY MARVYN IS MY STEPMOTHER. IN THIS PLACE I AM NOTHING. I DARE NOT RAISE MY VOICE, A SHADOW!" HER EYES GROW MOIST: "NEVER IN MY WHOLE LIFE HAVE I SET FOOT OUTSIDE THE CASTLE!"

NEXT MORNING THE SOUNDS FROM THE COURTYARD SIGNAL THE RETURN OF SIR LOWARY. DALE DESCENDS, BUT THIS TIME HE IS ARMED.

THERE HAS BEEN FIGHTING. SOME ARE MISSING, OTHERS WOUNDED, PACK HORSES ARE LOADED WITH GOODS. WITHOUT A DOUBT LOWARY HAS BEEN ON A RAID. AND FOR DALE THE SIMPLE TASK OF UNTANGLING AN INHERITANCE LOOMS AS A MAJOR PROBLEM.

NEXT WEEK—The Final Insult

1741

6-21

Prince Valiant
IN THE DAYS OF KING ARTHUR
BY HAROLD R FOSTER

Our Story:
SIR LOWARY STRIDES IN WITH ARROGANT MIEN, FRESH FROM A SUCCESSFUL RAID. THERE IS BLOOD ON HIS GARMENTS AND THE LUST OF BATTLE STILL IN HIS EYES. "SO, OUR LITTLE BOY-WARRIOR CARRIES HIS LADYLOVE'S FAVOR," HE SNEERS, POINTING AT ALETA'S TOKEN.

HE SNATCHES THE SCENTED TRIFLE FROM DALE'S BREAST AND BLOWS HIS NOSE VIOLENTLY INTO IT. FOR A BRIEF MOMENT DALE STANDS MOTIONLESS, ANGER RISING LIKE A COLD FLAME. HE WHIPS OUT HIS BRIGHT SWORD.

EVEN THE CASTLE WALLS SEEM TO SIGH WITH RELIEF.

NEXT WEEK— *Calm Before the Storm*

HAL FOSTER

LOWARY LEAPS BACK AND DRAWS. HE IS NO MEAN SWORDSMAN, BUT SUCH IS THE FURY OF DALE'S ATTACK THAT HE IS PUT ON THE DEFENSIVE.
SOMETHING TERRIBLE GLEAMS FROM HIS ADVERSARY'S EYES, A COLD AND DEADLY HATE THAT HIS INSULTS HAVE CREATED. HAS HE GONE TOO FAR? IS HE TO PAY FOR HIS MALICE? THE ANSWER COMES SUDDENLY.

1742

6-28

Prince Valiant

IN THE DAYS OF KING ARTHUR

BY HAROLD R FOSTER

Our Story: SO SIR LOWARY IS BURIED. THAT THERE WERE MORE SIGHS OF RELIEF THAN WAILING ATTESTED TO HIS POPULARITY.

ONLY AMONG SOME OF HIS HENCHMEN IS THERE ANY SORROW. "HE WAS SO SPLENDIDLY EVIL," THEY SAY. "WHERE CAN WE FIND ANOTHER LEADER HALF SO UNSCRUPULOUS?"

THE DEATH OF HER BROTHER-IN-LAW BRINGS A SURPRISING CHANGE IN LADY MARVYN. SHE THANKS DALE PROFUSELY, HOLDS HIS HAND, AND BECOMES ALMOST COY.

BUT IT IS MATILDA, THE STEPDAUGHTER, WHO DRESSES HIS WOUNDS. "MARVYN NOW RULES THE FIEF IN THE ABSENCE OF HER SON. IT IS RUMORED THAT HE IS DEAD. WHY, OTHERWISE, DID LOWARY MOVE IN?"

THE EVENING MEAL IS A GALA AFFAIR. LADY MARVYN WEARS HER BEST GOWN, LAUGHING, FLIRTING. MATILDA SITS QUIETLY, AS USUAL, SAYING NO WORD. THE LADY GETS QUITE TIPSY AND IS HELPED TO HER ROOM.

AFTER A LONG SILENCE, MATILDA SPEAKS: "MAY I STAY HERE WITH YOU FOR A WHILE? I HAVE NOTHING TO SAY, FOR I KNOW NOTHING OUTSIDE THIS GRIM PLACE. IT IS NICE TO JUST SIT HERE WITH YOU."

HE TELLS HER OF CAMELOT, THE JOUSTS, FAMOUS KNIGHTS AND JEWELED LADIES, AND SHE LISTENS WITH WIDE-EYED WONDER. DALE FINDS IT PLEASANT TO HAVE SUCH AN APPRECIATIVE AUDIENCE.

DALE DREAMS OF HIS LADY FAIR, ALETA THE UNATTAINABLE; WHILE MATILDA DREAMS OF SNUB-NOSED DALE MAKINNIE, SO BRAVE AND TERRIBLE IN BATTLE, YET SO KIND AND GENTLE.

NEXT WEEK — *The Awakening*

1743   7-5

Prince Valiant

IN THE DAYS OF KING ARTHUR

BY HAROLD R. FOSTER

Our Story: ACCORDING TO LAW, THE FIEF, ON THE DEATH OF ITS MASTER, WOULD PASS TO THE NEAREST MALE RELATIVE. LADY MARVYN MAKES HER PLANS. BY FAIR MEANS OR FOUL SHE INTENDS TO REMAIN MISTRESS OF MARVYN COURT.

SHE MUST HAVE A HUSBAND BEFORE SOME OTHER CLAIMANT ARRIVES. ARRAYED IN HER BEST FINERY SHE ENTERS, HER EYE ON DALE, HOPING FOR HIS APPROVAL.

SHE IS GAY AND CHARMING, EVEN BEAUTIFUL, BUT FOR THE SHREWD, HARD GLITTER IN HER EYES. MATILDA SITS SILENT, AS USUAL, AND IS SOON DISMISSED.

"THE MAN I CHOOSE AS A HUSBAND WILL RULE THIS CASTLE AND ALL ITS WIDE, FAIR LANDS. THE TAXES ALONE WILL MAKE HIM A MAN OF WEALTH AND IMPORTANCE."
"BUT WHAT OF YOUR SON?" ASKS DALE. "HE IS THE RIGHTFUL HEIR."

"OH, YES, POOR BABE," AND HERE SHE DABS HER EYES, "HE WAS ALWAYS A SICKLY CHILD, NOT LONG FOR THIS WORLD, I FEAR. HE WILL NEVER BE ABLE TO HANDLE THE FIEF."

DALE SEEKS OUT MATILDA, KNOWING SHE WILL GIVE HIM HONEST ANSWERS. "FEARING FOR THE SAFETY OF HER SON, LADY MARVYN TOOK HIM TO A MONASTERY, BUT WHICH ONE, NO ONE KNOWS EXCEPT HER LADYSHIP, AND SHE HAS KEPT THE SECRET WELL. RUMOR HAS IT THAT HE IS DEAD."

1744 © King Features Syndicate, Inc., 1970. World rights reserved. 7-12

AS THE ONLY YOUNG PEOPLE IN THE CASTLE THESE TWO NATURALLY FIND PLEASURE IN EACH OTHER'S COMPANY.

FROM THE DOORWAY ANGRY EYES OBSERVE THEM. DESPITE THE DIFFERENCE IN AGE, SHE HAS PLANNED TO WED DALE, AND IS ENRAGED THAT HE SHOULD FIND PLEASURE IN THE COMPANY OF HER DESPISED STEPCHILD!

NEXT WEEK—*The Three-Legged Table*

Prince Valiant
IN THE DAYS OF KING ARTHUR
BY HAROLD R. FOSTER

Our Story: LADY MARVYN HAS BUT ONE OVERPOWERING DESIRE: TO REMAIN MISTRESS OF THE FIEF. TO ACHIEVE THIS SHE MUST HAVE A HUSBAND, AND DALE MAKINNIE IS AT HAND. ONE PERSON STANDS IN THE WAY....

....MATILDA, HER DESPISED AND NEGLECTED STEPDAUGHTER. BUT, AS YOUTH CALLS TO YOUTH, SHE AND DALE ARE OFTEN TOGETHER..... THIS MUST STOP!

"JOIN ME IN THE SOLARIUM AND, OVER A REFRESHING CUP OF WINE, WE WILL DISCUSS FUTURE PLANS."

MATILDA AND DALE ARRIVE EARLY AND WHILE THEY WAIT: "LOOK, A LEG OF THE TABLE IS BEFORE EACH CHAIR, MOST UNCOMFORTABLE. LET US TURN THE TABLE."

THE LADY MARVYN TAKES HER CHAIR AND RAISES HER GOBLET: "NOW DRINK DEEP TO OUR FUTURE, MAY IT BE CROWNED WITH SUCCESS!" SHE STARES AT MATILDA, WAITING. THERE COMES A BEWILDERED LOOK IN HER EYES.

SOMEHOW SHE HAS BLUNDERED, AND HER WHITE FACE REVEALS THAT SHE NOW KNOWS WHAT IS IN STORE FOR HER. GRASPING A TABLE KNIFE SHE MAKES A DESPERATE LUNGE TOWARD MATILDA..... TOO LATE!

POISON! DALE AND MATILDA LOOK AT EACH OTHER HORRIFIED. THE FATAL GOBLET HAD BEEN MEANT FOR MATILDA, BUT WAS SET BEFORE LADY MARVYN WHEN THEY TURNED THE TABLE.

NEXT WEEK— *The New Mistress*

1745

7-19

1745

Prince Valiant

IN THE DAYS OF KING ARTHUR
BY Harold R. Foster

Our Story: DALE HAS BUT ONE DESIRE: TO COMPLETE THE KING'S MISSION AND LEAVE THIS DOLOROUS CASTLE WITH ITS HATREDS, CRUELTY AND DEATH FAR BEHIND.

AT LAST HE CAN EXAMINE THE RECORDS. THEY ARE ALL IN ORDER, AND MATILDA IS MISTRESS OF THE CASTLE UNTIL THE RIGHTFUL HEIR IS FOUND. BUT WHERE IS HE? LADY MARVYN HAS GONE TO HER GRAVE WITH THE SECRET.

"WHEN LADY MARVYN TOOK HER SON TO A MONASTERY SHE MUST HAVE HAD GUARDS OR SERVANTS TO ACCOMPANY HER. WE MUST FIND THEM. OUR SERVANTS AND THE VILLAGERS KNOW EVERYTHING THAT GOES ON IN THE CASTLE. PERHAPS IF YOU QUESTION THEM......?"

THE NEW MISTRESS CALLS IN THE ENTIRE STAFF AND GIVES INSTRUCTIONS, AND IT IS CLEAR THAT THE OLD SLIPSHOD DAYS ARE OVER. FLOORS ARE TO BE SCRUBBED, TAPESTRIES CLEANED, FURNITURE POLISHED; AND THE STEWARD, CHEF AND HOUSEKEEPER WHO ALLOWED THE MESS TO ACCUMULATE ARE DISCHARGED.

"WHILE MY FATHER LIVED THIS CASTLE WAS A BRIGHT AND ELEGANT PLACE. MY STEPMOTHER LET IT SINK INTO DECAY. I INTEND TO RESTORE IT, FOR IT IS THE ONLY PLACE I HAVE EVER KNOWN. NEVER HAVE I BEEN OUTSIDE THESE WALLS."

IN THE STABLES DALE FINDS ONE WHO WAS WITH LADY MARVYN WHEN SHE RODE AWAY WITH HER INFANT SON. "SHE TOOK HIM TO MEADOWSCARP AND PLACED HIM IN THE CARE OF THE GOOD BROTHERS. I KNOW THE WAY."

THEY RIDE FROM CASTLE MARVYN, DALE HOPING HE WILL NEVER SEE THE PLACE AGAIN, AND ANXIOUS TO RETURN TO CAMELOT AND TELL HIS STORY TO HIS LADY FAIR, QUEEN ALETA.

WHILE MATILDA, WIDE-EYED WITH WONDER, RIDES CLOSE TO DALE, FRIGHTENED BY THIS STRANGE, UNFAMILIAR WORLD.

NEXT WEEK — *The Dependent*

HAL FOSTER

Prince Valiant
IN THE DAYS OF KING ARTHUR
BY HAROLD R FOSTER

Our Story: ON THIS, HER FIRST VENTURE INTO THE WORLD BEYOND THE CASTLE WALLS, MATILDA IS FILLED WITH VAGUE FEARS. ONLY THE PRESENCE OF DALE REASSURES HER.

A STORMY NIGHT, FAR FROM ANY HABITATION, AND DALE CONTRIVES A SIMPLE SHELTER. THIS IS THE FIRST TIME MATILDA HAS BEEN EXPOSED TO THE ELEMENTS, AND HER STALWART PROTECTOR HAS BROUGHT COMFORT.

HER HELPLESSNESS ANNOYS DALE. SHE DEPENDS ON HIM FOR EVERYTHING. HE COMPARES HER, UNFAVORABLY, WITH QUEEN ALETA, HIS LADY IN DOMNEI.

NOT BEING USED TO HORSES, IT IS PREDICTABLE THAT SHE SHOULD FALL OFF. WHILE CROSSING A FORD SHE DOES THE EXPECTED THING. DALE SWEARS AND MATILDA BURSTS INTO TEARS. SHE LOOKS SO PATHETIC HE HAS TO COMFORT HER.

THEY COME AT LAST TO MEADOWSCARP AND THE END OF DALE'S MISSION: TO LEARN IF THE REAL HEIR TO THE FIEF AND MARVYN CASTLE IS ALIVE OR DEAD. EITHER WAY DALE WILL BE FREE TO RETURN TO CAMELOT.

AFTER MUCH HAMMERING A WICKET OPENS AND A MONK ASKS THEIR BUSINESS. THEY ARE FINALLY ADMITTED AND LED BEFORE THE KINDLY ABBOT.

THE RECORDS ARE BROUGHT OUT. "YES, THE SON OF THE LATE LORD MARVYN WAS BROUGHT HERE FOR SAFEKEEPING BY HIS MOTHER," RELATES THE ABBOT. "IT WAS ON A NIGHT OF COLD AND RAIN AND THE CHILD CAUGHT A COLD AND DIED A FEW DAYS LATER." AND IT IS THUS THAT THE MYSTERY OF MARVYN CASTLE CLOSES.

NEXT WEEK— Or Does It?

HAL FOSTER

1747

8-2

Prince Valiant
IN THE DAYS OF KING ARTHUR
BY HAROLD R FOSTER

Our Story: DALE MAKINNIE SIGHS WITH RELIEF AS THE LAST DETAILS OF HIS MISSION ARE COMPLETED AND HE IS FREE TO RETURN TO THE SPLENDORS OF CAMELOT.

WITH THE ABBOT'S BLESSING THEY LEAVE THE MONASTERY. DALE SETS A FAST PACE, FOR BUT A DAY'S RIDE WILL BRING THEM TO A CROSSROAD WHERE HE WILL BE RID OF HIS HELPLESS CHARGE....SHE TO RETURN TO MARVYN CASTLE, HE TO CAMELOT.

IN HIS EAGERNESS HE HAD FORGOTTEN HIS KNIGHTLY DUTY.... CAN HE LEAVE THIS FRIGHTENED MAID TO MAKE THE LONG JOURNEY HOME WITH ONLY ONE AGING GUARD TO PROTECT HER? NO! HE MUST TAKE HER WITH HIM.

CAMELOT! CASTLE OF WONDER, HOME OF HEROES. HERE HE WILL STAND BEFORE THE KING AND DELIVER HIS REPORT. AND HERE HE WILL REQUEST A GUARD TO CONDUCT MATILDA BACK TO CASTLE MARVYN IN SAFETY.

THE MOMENT HE HAS DREAMED OF: HE STANDS BEFORE THE KING AND GIVES AN ACCOUNT OF HIS MISSION. AND THE KING NODS HIS APPROVAL, BUT HIS KEEN EYES TELL HIM MORE THAN THE WORDS.

THE AUDIENCE ENDS AND PRINCE ARN IS THE FIRST TO WELCOME HIM BACK: "COME TO DINNER TONIGHT AND BRING THE LADY MATILDA THAT WE MAY HEAR OF YOUR ADVENTURE."

BUT IT IS MATILDA, STARRY-EYED AND BREATHLESS, WHO TELLS THE STORY. NO KNIGHT IN SHINING ARMOR EVER EXCEEDED DALE IN COURAGE, WISDOM AND HARDIHOOD. "HE SHOULD BE KNIGHTED AND GIVEN A SEAT AT THE ROUND TABLE," SHE CONCLUDES.

"WHEN LORD MARVYN HELD THE FIEF IT WAS A STRONG POINT ON OUR NORTHERN MARCHES," MUSES ARTHUR. "WE MUST FIND THE MAID MATILDA A SUITABLE HUSBAND WHO WILL RESTORE ITS STRENGTH."

NEXT WEEK— *But Who, Sire?*

HAL FOSTER

1748   © King Features Syndicate, Inc., 1970. World rights reserved   8-9

Prince Valiant

IN THE DAYS OF KING ARTHUR
BY HAROLD R. FOSTER

Our Story: ALETA TAKES PITY ON MATILDA, SHE LOOKS SO PATHETIC IN HER PLAIN GOWN AND THREADBARE CLOAK. A CHANGE OF COSTUME MIGHT ENHANCE HER PLAIN LOOKS.

THE COURT IS A FABULOUS PLACE, BETTER BY FAR THAN ANY OF THE FAIRY TALES SHE HAS READ, AND THE WONDER OF IT ALL MAKES HER FACE GLOW. "ONCE UPON A TIME I WAS YOUNG LIKE THAT," MUSES ALETA, A TINY BIT JEALOUS.

FROM THE GALLERY DALE'S EYES FOLLOW ALETA, THE MOST BEAUTIFUL OF WOMEN, WITH GRACE, POISE.... AND WHO IS THE LOVELY GIRL BESIDE HER? CAN IT BE....? YES, IT IS MATILDA!

MANY A GAY YOUNG KNIGHT FINDS HER FRANK INNOCENCE REFRESHING, AND THEY CLAMOR FOR HER ATTENTION. "STUPID GIRL," MUTTERS DALE, "TOO IGNORANT TO SEE THEY ARE JUST PLAYING WITH HER. THEIR INTENTIONS ARE NOT AS FINE AS THEIR WORDS."

"YOU KNOW NOTHING OF THE WORLD, SO DON'T ENCOURAGE THOSE GAY BLADES WHO CHASE AFTER YOU," ADMONISHES DALE. "YOU ARE MY RESPONSIBILITY UNTIL SAFELY BACK IN MARVYN CASTLE." MATILDA SAYS NOTHING BUT GAZES UP INTO HIS FACE ADORINGLY.

UNDER ALETA'S TUTELAGE MATILDA LEARNS QUICKLY. SHE EVEN ATTEMPTS A FLIRTATION OR TWO, AND LAUGHS AT HER OWN INEPTNESS.....

..... WHILE DALE, SWEARING UNDER HIS BREATH, WATCHES FROM A DISTANCE AND WISHES SHE WOULD GO HOME AND SO RELIEVE HIM OF HIS TROUBLESOME DUTY.

WHY IS IT THAT MARRIED WOMEN HATE TO SEE A CONTENTED BACHELOR WANDERING AROUND FREE? THEY JUST MUST FIND HIM A BRIDE SO HE WILL 'GET MARRIED AND SETTLE DOWN!' WHO WANTS TO SETTLE DOWN?

NEXT WEEK — Not Dale!

1749

8-16

Prince Valiant
IN THE DAYS OF KING ARTHUR
BY HAROLD R FOSTER

Our Story: ALETA IS NEVER SO HAPPY AS WHEN SHE SITS QUIETLY AMID THE DIN OF HER ROBUST FAMILY. THERE IS MUCH LOVE THERE, EVEN THOUGH IT DOES SOUND LIKE A RIOT. EVERYONE, SHE DECIDES, SHOULD BE HAPPILY MARRIED. DALE AND MATILDA, FOR INSTANCE.

FIRST SHE MUST CURE DALE OF HIS INFATUATION FOR HER. SO SHE DEMANDS NUMEROUS SERVICES, MENIAL TASKS THAT MAKE IT PLAIN THAT SHE IS A QUEEN, HE BUT A WARRIOR NOT YET KNIGHTED.

HE LEAVES HIS ADORED LADY, FEELING VERY SMALL, BUT IN THE COMPANY OF MATILDA HIS CONFIDENCE IS RESTORED. HER EVERY GLANCE TELLS HIM HE IS THE MOST WONDERFUL HERO IN THE WORLD.

HE BROUGHT HER TO CAMELOT, THEREFORE HE FEELS RESPONSIBLE FOR HER SAFETY. ONE SO PRETTY, TRUSTING AND INNOCENT IS SURE TO BE A TARGET FOR PLAYFUL YOUNG MEN. AND IS!

AND DALE, WHO HAS BEEN SO CALM IN THE FACE OF DANGER, FLIES INTO A RAGE AT THIS TRIFLE, AND THE AFFAIR WOULD END IN A DUEL BUT FOR SIR GAWAIN. "IF YOU STOP YOUNG MEN FROM KISSING PRETTY GIRLS, YOU WILL UPSET THE WHOLE HUMAN RACE," HE SCOLDS.

"OH, DALE, I AM SO SORRY. EVER SINCE WE MET I HAVE BEEN A NUISANCE. YOU RESTORED TO ME MY CASTLE AND LANDS, BUT I HAVE GIVEN YOU NOTHING BUT TROUBLE."

"I WILL LEAVE CAMELOT AT DAWN. THE KING WILL GIVE ME A GUARD, NEVER MORE WILL I......." SHE NEVER FINISHES THE SENTENCE, BUT IT DOESN'T MATTER. IT WAS UNIMPORTANT.

1750 © King Features Syndicate, Inc. 1970. World rights reserved. 8-23

"OH, WASN'T IT ROMANTIC," SAYS ALETA WITH A SMUG GRIN.
"ABOUT AS ROMANTIC AS A HUNGRY PIKE SWALLOWING HOOK, LINE AND SINKER!" ANSWERS VAL.

NEXT WEEK—The Ready-made Knight

HAL FOSTER

Prince Valiant

IN THE DAYS OF KING ARTHUR

BY Harold R. Foster

Our Story: ALETA GETS A SCOLDING: "DUE TO YOUR MEDDLING, DALE AND MATILDA ARE MARRIED AND ABOUT TO 'SETTLE DOWN.' POOR DALE, HE CAME TO CAMELOT TO EARN HIS SPURS, NOT TO BE HALTERED BY THE BONDS OF MATRIMONY." "I CAN ARRANGE A KNIGHTHOOD TOO," ANSWERS ALETA CHEERFULLY.

SHE GOES STRAIGHT TO THE KING: "SIRE, DALE MAKINNIE, NOW MARRIED TO MATILDA, IS THE NEW MASTER OF MARVYN CASTLE AND FIEF. BUT HE IS WITHOUT TITLE, AND SO WILL HAVE NO AUTHORITY AS COMMANDER OF THE GARRISON."
"SEND HIM IN," GROWLS ARTHUR.

A SIMPLE CEREMONY, HELD IN THE KING'S DRESSING ROOM, BUT THE SHINING BLADE OF FAMED EXCALIBUR TOUCHES DALE ON EACH SHOULDER.... "ARISE, DALE MAKINNIE, KNIGHT, MASTER OF MARVYN AND ALL THE LANDS."

AS DIRECTOR AND PRODUCER OF THIS ROMANTIC SKETCH ALETA PROVIDES A BANQUET. NOT TO BE OUTDONE, MATILDA ARISES: "YOU ARE ALL INVITED TO A HUNT AT MARVYN CASTLE. THE FOREST HAS BEEN UNTOUCHED FOR YEARS AND IS TEEMING WITH GAME."

WHEN THE PARTY LEAVES CAMELOT THE FIRST SNOW OF WINTER IS FALLING, DISCOURAGING MANY, SO THAT ONLY THE KEENEST HUNTERS GO ALONG, AMONG THEM PRINCE ARN.

"I HOPE THIS SNOW WILL NOT HINDER THE HUNT," SAYS THE NEW LADY MATILDA MAKINNIE. "DUE TO THE MISMANAGEMENT OF MY STEPMOTHER THE LARDER IS EMPTY AND WE WILL NEED ALL THE VENISON WE CAN GET TO SEE US THROUGH THE WINTER."

NO LONGER IS MARVYN CASTLE A DARK AND SINISTER PLACE. LIGHTS SHINE FROM EVERY WINDOW, SONG AND LAUGHTER RING OUT, AND THE SERFS ARE HOPEFUL THAT THE OLD DAYS HAVE RETURNED.

8-30 © King Features Syndicate, Inc., 1970. World rights reserved. 1751

ARN FINDS A COMPANION WHO LOVES THE DANGEROUS SPORT OF BOAR HUNTING AND, IN THEIR EXCITEMENT THEY LOSE ALL SENSE OF TIME AND DIRECTION.

NEXT WEEK— Lost!

HAL FOSTER

Our Story: PRINCE ARN AND HIS HUNTING COMPANION TRACK DOWN THE WILD BOAR AND BRING IT TO BAY. ARN ADVANCES, SPEAR AT THE READY, AND WITH GROWLS AND SHOUTS TRIES TO INFURIATE THE DANGEROUS BEAST INTO CHARGING.

WITH A SCREAM OF RAGE IT CHARGES. ARN KNEELS ON THE BUTT OF HIS SPEAR AND MEETS THE IMPACT. THE FIERCE BEAST WOULD HAVE CHARGED RIGHT UP THE SPEAR BUT FOR THE STOUT CROSSPIECE.

WITH A MIGHTY HEAVE ARN TURNS THE TUSKER OVER ON ITS BACK AND DELIVERS THE FINISHING STROKE.

IT IS GROWING DARK AND A RISING WIND WARNS THAT THE DAY'S HUNT IS OVER. A BLAST ON THE HORN SHOULD BRING THE SERVANTS TO CARRY IN THE GAME, BUT NO ONE RESPONDS.

THEY FOLLOW THEIR TRAIL BACK, BUT DRIFTING SNOW SOON OBSCURES THEIR TRACKS. "WELL, WE ARE LOST," ARN REMARKS CHEERFULLY. "THE STORM IS INCREASING, AND IF WE DON'T FIND SHELTER BEFORE NIGHTFALL WE ARE IN A BAD WAY."

"LOOK, A CASTLE!" CRIES ARN AND, SETTING SPURS TO HIS WEARY HORSE, GALLOPS DOWN THE HILLSIDE. HIS COMPANION SHOUTS A WARNING THAT ARN DOES NOT HEAR.

HE WATCHES IN HORROR AS ARN GALLOPS ALONG THE CAUSEWAY. SILENTLY THE GREAT GATES OPEN, HE ENTERS, AND THE GATES CLANG SHUT LIKE THE JAWS OF A TRAP.

HAL FOSTER

1752 (C) King Features Syndicate, Inc., 1970. World rights reserved. 9-6

THE MORNING IS WELL ADVANCED BEFORE HE FINDS HIS WAY BACK TO MARVYN CASTLE AND GIVES THE ALARM. "PRINCE ARN HAS ENTERED CHARIOT GARDE AND IS NOW IN THE HANDS OF MORGAN LE FAY, THE SORCERESS!"

NEXT WEEK—The Spider and The Fly

Prince Valiant

IN THE DAYS OF KING ARTHUR

By Harold R Foster

Our Story: TO FIND SHELTER FROM THE STORM PRINCE ARN ENTERS A FORBIDDING CASTLE. THE GATES OPEN TO HIM AND CLOSE BEHIND HIM. IN THE COURTYARD A SILENT FIGURE TAKES HIS HORSE AND GESTURES FOR HIM TO ENTER.

AND IN SILENCE HE IS TAKEN BEFORE HIS HOSTESS. A TREMOR OF FEAR RUNS UP HIS SPINE AS HE RECOGNIZES MORGAN LE FAY, SISTER OF ARTHUR AND THE MOST FEARED SORCERESS IN BRITAIN.

SHE MOTIONS TO THE SERVANTS TO REMOVE HIS SAXE-KNIFE. "SATAN IS INDEED GOOD TO ME IN SENDING SUCH A GIFT!" SHE LAUGHS, POINTING TO THE CREST ON HIS TUNIC.

"THE CRIMSON STALLION, CREST OF PRINCE VALIANT. SO YOU MUST BE HIS SON, PRINCE ARN. HOW DELIGHTFUL WILL BE MY REVENGE ON THAT PROUD, OVERBEARING AND OH! SO VIRTUOUS FATHER OF YOURS! THE FIENDS WILL REJOICE!"

WHEN THE WORD COMES TO MARVYN CASTLE THAT ARN WAS SEEN ENTERING CHARIOT GARDE, DALE WASTES NO TIME IN DESPATCHING SWIFT RIDERS TO NOTIFY PRINCE VALIANT OF HIS SON'S DANGER. A DANGER THAT WOULD BE MULTIPLIED SHOULD AN ATTACK BE MADE.

PRINCE VALIANT SEEMS CALM AS HE RECEIVES THE MESSAGE. NO ONE WOULD EVER KNOW HOW CLOSE HE IS TO PANIC. BUT THE PRESENCE OF DANGER IS ALWAYS A TONIC TO HIM, CLEARING HIS MIND, SHARPENING HIS WITS. SLOWLY A PLAN DEVELOPS.

HE SEEKS OUT THE KING AND REQUESTS THE KEY TO MERLIN'S LABORATORY. EVER SINCE THAT NIGHT AT DOZMARY POND WHEN NIMUE, THE WATER MAIDEN, LED MERLIN TO HIS STRANGE DOOM, THESE ROOMS HAVE BEEN LOCKED.

BUT VAL HAD BEEN MERLIN'S FAVORITE PUPIL, AND SO THE KING GRANTS HIS REQUEST.

NEXT WEEK—*Into the Trap*

1753   9-13

Prince Valiant
IN THE DAYS OF KING ARTHUR
BY Harold R Foster

Our Story: IN A DUNGEON CELL PRINCE ARN AWAITS THE FATE MORGAN LE FAY IS PLANNING FOR HIM. HE EXPECTS THE WORST, FOR HIS FATHER HAD THWARTED ONE OF HER EVIL SCHEMES, AND SHE THIRSTS FOR REVENGE.

IN MERLIN'S LABORATORY VAL STUDIES THE TWO HUGE VOLUMES TITLED 'HOCUS' AND 'POCUS' IN WHICH THE WISE PHILOSOPHER HAD WRITTEN THE SECRETS OF HIS MAGIC.

MERLIN, A MAN OF GREAT WISDOM, HAD FOUND THAT MEN DID NOT LISTEN TO WORDS OF WISDOM, SO HE INVENTED AND PRACTICED THE TRICKS OF MAGIC THAT PUZZLED AND FRIGHTENED HIS LISTENERS. AS A GREAT WIZARD HIS WORDS BORE WEIGHT.

MORGAN LE FAY, THE SORCERESS, PRACTICES WITH DRUGS. SURROUNDED BY HER WITCHES, SHE BREWS POTIONS FROM HENBANE, TOADSTOOLS, NIGHTSHADE AND OTHER OMINOUS MATERIALS. THE CONDITION OF THE SERVANTS AND SLAVES SHE HAS PRACTICED ON IS THE HORRID RESULT OF HER EXPERIMENTS.

NOW VAL DONS MERLIN'S ROBE WITH ITS SECRET POCKETS, HIDDEN STRINGS AND WIRES, VIALS OF CHEMICALS, AND BEFORE A MIRROR PRACTICES A FEW DECEPTIONS. ONE WOULD THINK HE WAS CALMLY PREPARING FOR AN ENTERTAINMENT INSTEAD OF A CONTEST FOR HIS SON'S VERY LIFE.

NOW HE FINDS RELIEF FROM ANXIETY IN ACTION. MOUNTED ON ARVAK AND LEADING A SPARE HORSE HE SETS OUT FOR CHARIOT GARDE TO PIT HIS POOR MAGIC AGAINST LE FAY'S SORCERY FOR ARN'S LIFE.

FAR OUT IN THE FROZEN MARSH STANDS THE CASTLE, DARK AND FORBIDDING. VAL PAYS A PEASANT TO CARE FOR THE HORSES, DONS MERLIN'S ROBE, AND SETS FOOT UPON THE CAUSEWAY.

1754   © King Features Syndicate, Inc., 1970. World rights reserved.   9-20

LE FAY IS OVERJOYED. PRINCE VALIANT IS WALKING INTO A FATE SHE HAS LONG PLANNED. HOW SWEET WILL BE HER REVENGE!

NEXT WEEK — *The Viper*

HAL FOSTER

Our Story: PRINCE VALIANT IS USHERED INTO THE PRESENCE OF MORGAN LE FAY, THERE TO PIT HIS AMATEURISH MAGIC AGAINST HER SORCERY. AND THE PRIZE? HIS SON'S LIFE!

"GREETINGS, LE FAY, TIME HAS NOT FLAWED YOUR BEAUTY. IT IS EIGHTEEN YEARS TO THE DAY SINCE I FIRST CAME HERE TO RELEASE SIR GAWAIN. I HAD HOPED THAT YOU HAD LEARNED A LESSON."

THE HATE THAT GLEAMS FROM HER EYES TURNS TO WIDE-EYED HORROR. A VIPER SLITHERS OUT OF VAL'S SLEEVE AND STARES AT HER WITH UNBLINKING TOPAZ EYES. "COME BACK, ALICE, IT IS NOT YET TIME," COAXES VAL, AS HE FUMBLES IN HIS ROBE FOR THE RIGHT STRING AND WISHES HE HAD SPENT MORE TIME IN PRACTICE.

"ALICE IS IMPATIENT," HE EXPLAINS. "SHE IS OVERCHARGED WITH VENOM, BUT I WILL LET HER LOOSE TONIGHT THAT SHE MAY FIND RELIEF. SHE ONLY STRIKES IN THE DARK, SO LET US HAVE LIGHT." AND VAL SNAPS HIS FINGERS, A FLAME APPEARS, AND HE LIGHTS THE CANDLES.

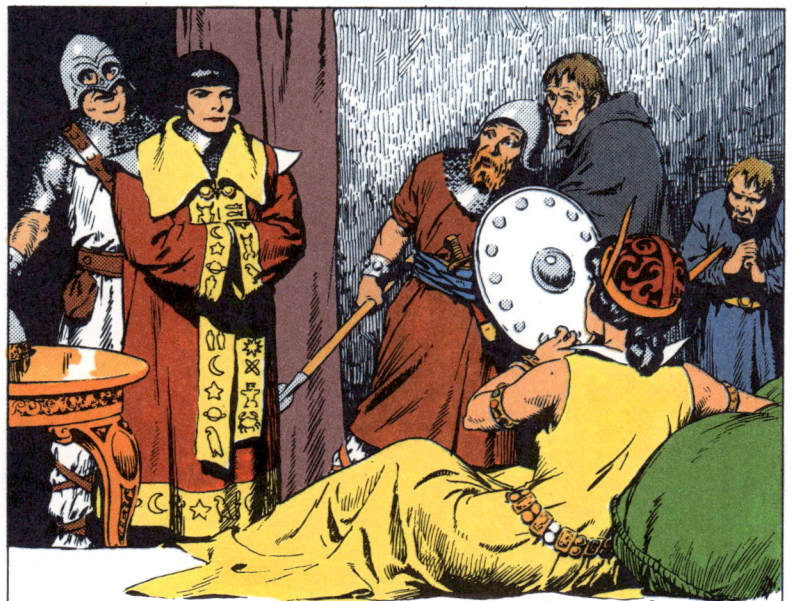

THE FLAME GOES OUT, LEAVING THE SMELL OF SULPHUR AND BURNT FLESH IN THE AIR. TRICKERY, BUT HE IS SATISFIED WITH THE RESULT: FEAR! FEAR WILL DULL THEIR THINKING, WELL WORTH THE PRICE OF SEARED FINGERS.

LE FAY IS FIRST TO REGAIN HER COMPOSURE. "SUCH TRICKS MY JUGGLERS PERFORM TO AMUSE DINNER GUESTS. NOW SEE SOME OF MINE: DARG, AWAKEN!"

A HEAP OF RAGS IN A CORNER MOVES, A FACE APPEARS, BUT SUCH A FACE! BLANK, GRINNING, WITHOUT HUMOR OR FEELING....... NOT EVEN MADNESS!

"DARG!" SHE SCREAMS, POINTING AT VAL, "KILL!"

NEXT WEEK— The Thing

1755 © King Features Syndicate, Inc., 1970. World rights reserved. 9-27

HAL FOSTER

Prince Valiant
IN THE DAYS OF KING ARTHUR
BY HAROLD R FOSTER

Our Story: PRINCE VALIANT AND MORGAN LE FAY CONTEND FOR THE LIFE OF ARN. VAL, BY USING SOME OF MERLIN'S MAGIC TRICKS, INSTILLS FEAR. THE SORCERESS COUNTERS BY CALLING UPON DARG.

"*KILL!*" SHE ORDERS. THE HORRIBLE, MINDLESS CREATURE ADVANCES, UNARMED, BUT HIS HUGE HANDS REACH OUT TO TEAR, TO STRANGLE. VAL KNOCKS HIM DOWN.

HE ARISES, STILL SMILING VACANTLY, WITHOUT FEELING, INTENT ONLY ON OBEYING HIS MISTRESS'S COMMAND.

TIME AND TIME AGAIN HE IS FELLED. VAL DRAWS HIS KNIFE. IT WOULD BE MERCIFUL TO PUT AN END TO THIS CREATION OF LE FAY'S ART.

"*ENOUGH, DARG, COME GET YOUR REWARD.*" IT CRAWLS TO HER SIDE AND SHE DIPS A BISCUIT INTO A SMALL JAR AND GIVES IT TO HIM. "*HASHEESH!*" SHE EXPLAINS, "*HE LOVES IT AND NOW HE WILL SLEEP HAPPILY UNTIL I NEED HIM AGAIN.*"

"*AND THIS IS THE FATE I HAVE PLANNED FOR YOUR SON, TO BE MY IDIOT SLAVE AS LONG AS I LIVE.*"
"*THAT MAY NOT BE LONG,*" VAL REPLIES, AS THE VIPER CRAWLS OUT ON HIS HAND. "*BRING HIM FORTH!*"

"*DID YOU CALL ME, FATHER?*" VAL TURNS AND THERE, STANDING IN THE DOORWAY, IS ARN.

1756   © King Features Syndicate, Inc., 1970. World rights reserved.   10-4

ALTHOUGH HIS HEART BEATS WILDLY, VAL REMAINS OUTWARDLY CALM. "*YES, I DID, SON. WHAT KEPT YOU SO LONG?*"

NEXT WEEK— *History Repeats*

Prince Valiant
IN THE DAYS OF KING ARTHUR
BY HAROLD R. FOSTER

Our Story: PRINCE ARN STANDS GRINNING IN THE DOORWAY. THIS IS STRANGE, FOR HE IS SUPPOSED TO LIE CHAINED IN A NOISOME DUNGEON. TERROR SHOWS IN THE EYES OF MORGAN LE FAY. ONLY BY MAGIC COULD HE HAVE ESCAPED.

"WE TAKE OUR LEAVE OF YOUR QUESTIONABLE HOSPITALITY." HERE VAL FUMBLES FOR THE RIGHT STRING, FINDS IT AND THE VIPER SLIDES OUT ON HIS PALM. "I LEAVE ALICE HERE; SHE STRIKES ONLY IN THE DARK; BE CAREFUL WHEN PASSING THE SPOT WHERE SHE WILL BE WAITING."

"NOW! HOW IN HEAVEN'S NAME DID YOU ESCAPE FROM THAT DUNGEON?" WONDERS VAL. "YOU ARRIVED JUST IN TIME, FOR I WAS RUNNING OUT OF MAGIC TRICKS."

THERE IS NO PURSUIT, FOR LE FAY HAS ORDERED A SEARCH FOR THE LETHAL GUEST. FEAR WILL HAUNT THE CASTLE FOR MANY DAYS TO COME.

IT IS NOT UNTIL THEY ARE MOUNTED AND ARE A SAFE DISTANCE AWAY FROM PURSUIT THAT ARN TELLS THE STORY OF HIS ESCAPE.

"WHEN I WAS SMALL I LOVED TO LISTEN TO THE STORIES GEOFFREY, OUR HISTORIAN, USED TO TELL, AND MY FAVORITE WAS THE ONE WHERE YOU ESCAPED FROM LE FAY'S CASTLE AND RESCUED SIR GAWAIN....."

"....THE CELL WHERE I WAS CHAINED FITTED GEOFFREY'S TALE IN EVERY DETAIL..... IT WAS THE SAME CELL!...."

"....I REMEMBERED THAT YOU USED YOUR BELT BUCKLE. BY GRINDING THE TONGUE DOWN ON THE STONES I FASHIONED A PICK AND WENT TO WORK ON THE LOCK....."

NEXT WEEK—*Monkey See, Monkey Do'*

1757

10-11

1757

Prince Valiant
IN THE DAYS OF KING ARTHUR
BY HAROLD R. FOSTER

Our Story: PRINCE ARN CONTINUES THE STORY OF HIS ESCAPE: "MANY TIMES HAD GEOFFREY, THE HISTORIAN, TOLD THE TALE OF HOW YOU ESCAPED FROM MORGAN LE FAY'S DUNGEON. I REMEMBERED EVERY DETAIL.... THE CELL IN WHICH YOU HAD BEEN IMPRISONED WAS THE SAME IN WHICH I FOUND MYSELF....

"...BUT AFTER EIGHTEEN YEARS THE BARS WERE RUSTED FIRMLY IN PLACE. I DISMANTLED THE COT AND USED ONE OF ITS TIMBERS TO APPLY FORCE. FINALLY THE LINTEL YOU HAD SO PAINSTAKINGLY LOOSENED MOVED AND THE BARS CAME FREE...

"AFTER CLIMBING OUT I CLUNG TO THE SILL AND, EVEN AS YOU HAD DONE, REPLACED THE BARS AND LINTEL, THEN DROPPED TO THE FROZEN MARSH.....

"THE ICE WAS FIRM ALONG THE NORTH WALL AND I FELT QUITE PROUD OF MYSELF. I HAD ESCAPED FROM LE FAY'S DUNGEON! THEN I REMEMBERED THAT I WAS BUT FOLLOWING MY FATHER'S PATH, STEP BY STEP.

"AS I CAME TO THE FRONT OF THE CASTLE, YOU WERE CROSSING THE DRAWBRIDGE. I DID NOT RECOGNIZE YOU UNTIL TOO LATE, FOR YOU WERE WEARING MERLIN'S GOWN. I DARED NOT SWIM TO THE CAUSEWAY, FOR WATCHMEN IN THE TOWERS WOULD SEE ME.

"THE BRIDGE WAS UP BUT IT WAS EASY TO SCALE THE TIMBERS. I FELT BETTER, FOR I WAS NO LONGER FOLLOWING IN MY FATHER'S FOOTSTEPS. NOW I WAS ON MY OWN.

"ENTERING BY THE CHAINPORT I FUMBLED MY WAY ALONG THE GLOOMY HALLS AND AT LAST FOUND LE FAY'S SOLAR.

HAL FOSTER

"I TRUST, SIRE, THAT MY ENTRANCE WAS AT THE MOST DRAMATIC MOMENT. BY THE EXPRESSION ON OUR HOSTESS'S FACE I WOULD PREDICT THAT SHE WILL HESITATE TO PUT YOUR MAGIC TO THE TEST AGAIN!"

NEXT WEEK–The Merry Huntress

Prince Valiant
IN THE DAYS OF KING ARTHUR
BY HAROLD R. FOSTER

Our Story: PRINCE VALIANT AND HIS SON ARN RIDE AWAY FROM CHARIOT GARDE AND THE MALICE OF MORGAN LE FAY. "A FEW DAYS IN A DUNGEON MAKES ME APPRECIATE THE FRESH AIR AND SUNSHINE," REMARKS ARN, TAKING A DEEP BREATH.

THEY ARE BOTH TIRED AND HUNGRY AND SET A FAST PACE TOWARD MARVYN CASTLE. "I WONDER IF THE HUNT IS STILL IN PROGRESS," SAYS ARN HOPEFULLY. "I WOULD ENJOY A FEW DAYS OF SPORT."

DALE MAKINNIE AND HIS BRIDE MATILDA GIVE THEM A WARM WELCOME.

THE HUNT IS STILL FAR FROM OVER AND A MERRY THRONG IS GATHERED IN THE GREAT HALL. EVERYONE HAS A TALE TO TELL OF THE DAY'S HUNT, AND ARN IS EAGER TO STAY AND MAKE UP FOR THE DAYS LOST THROUGH HIS IMPRISONMENT IN CHARIOT GARDE.

BUT VAL IS STILL ON DUTY IN CAMELOT AND MUST RETURN AT ONCE. DALE MAKES A REQUEST: "EARL DONAT HAS BEEN SLASHED BY A WILD BOAR AND MUST STAY UNTIL HIS WOUND HEALS. WILL YOU BE SO KIND AS TO ESCORT LADY DONAT BACK TO CAMELOT?"

VAL WISHES ARN GOOD HUNTING AND RIDES AWAY... AND LADY DONAT SMILES; IT WILL BE PLEASANT TO RIDE WITH A HANDSOME AND FAMOUS KNIGHT INSTEAD OF HER GRUMPY OLD HUSBAND.

SHE IS A GAY AND WITTY COMPANION AND A GOOD HORSEWOMAN, BUT A RECKLESS ONE. MORE THAN ONCE VAL WARNS HER OF THE SLIPPERY FOOTING.

BUT SHE WILLFULLY GALLOPS DOWN TO A FORD JUST FOR THE THRILL THAT DANGER BRINGS.

NEXT WEEK—*Trouble comes Double*

1759

10-25

HAL FOSTER

Prince Valiant
IN THE DAYS OF KING ARTHUR
BY HAROLD R. FOSTER

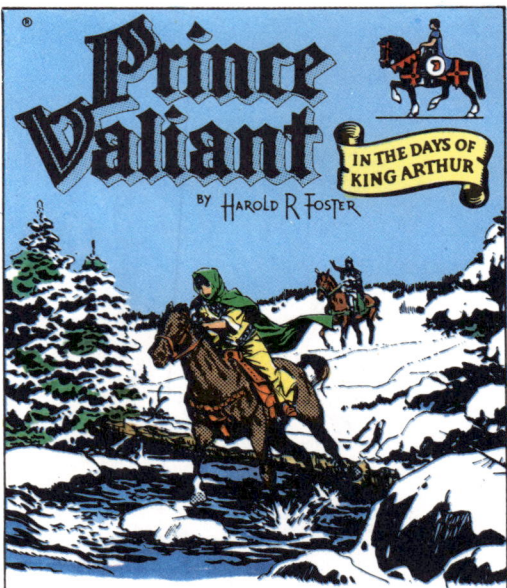

Our Story: IT IS PRINCE VALIANT'S DUTY TO ESCORT THE LADY DONAT BACK TO CAMELOT, AND HE FINDS IT A PLEASANT ASSIGNMENT. SHE IS YOUNG AND GAY, BUT WILLFUL. DESPITE HIS WARNING SHE APPROACHES A FORD AT FULL GALLOP.

HER MOUNT SLIPS ON THE ICY ROCKS, TRIES TO RISE, SCREAMS AND LIES STILL. LADY DONAT ARISES SLOWLY, SHAKEN BUT UNHARMED.

"A BROKEN NECK. YOU WILL HAVE TO RIDE DOUBLE WITH ME ON ARVAK UNTIL WE CAN FIND YOU ANOTHER HORSE."

HER GARMENTS ARE WET, THE WIND COLD, SO SHE CLINGS CLOSELY TO VAL FOR WARMTH. VERY CLOSE... BUT, THEN, FOR YEARS SHE HAS BEEN MARRIED TO A QUARRELSOME OLD MAN...

IN A TINY HAMLET THEY FIND SHELTER FOR THE NIGHT. IT IS IN A POOR DISTRICT AND THERE ARE NO HORSES FOR SALE. LADY DONAT, LIKE A TRUE SPORT, MAKES NO COMPLAINT.

AT HER SUGGESTION, VAL ADJUSTS THE HARNESS AND SETS THE SADDLE FARTHER BACK SO SHE CAN SIT COMFORTABLY IN FRONT.

IT IS MUCH MORE PLEASANT TO RIDE THIS WAY. HE WISHES IT COULD BE ALETA WHO IS CLINGING SO CLOSE TO HIM. HOWEVER, IT IS NOT, SO WHY NOT MAKE THE BEST OF IT. AS HE HAS NO INTENTION OF BECOMING INVOLVED WITH LADY DONAT, HE EVEN FEELS QUITE VIRTUOUS.

OFTEN HAS ALETA CLIMBED TO THE WATCHTOWER TO GAZE UP THE ROAD BY WHICH VAL WILL RETURN FROM ANOTHER OF HIS HIGH-HEARTED ADVENTURES.

NEXT WEEK – The End of Romance

1760   © King Features Syndicate, Inc., 1970. World rights reserved.   11-1

Prince Valiant
IN THE DAYS OF KING ARTHUR
BY HAROLD R FOSTER

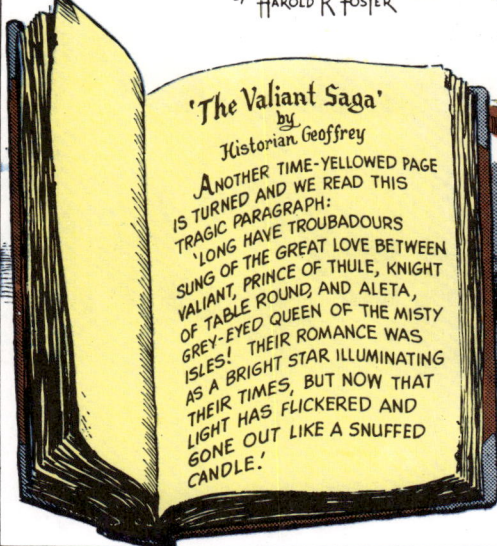

'The Valiant Saga' by Historian Geoffrey

ANOTHER TIME-YELLOWED PAGE IS TURNED AND WE READ THIS TRAGIC PARAGRAPH: 'LONG HAVE TROUBADOURS SUNG OF THE GREAT LOVE BETWEEN VALIANT, PRINCE OF THULE, KNIGHT OF TABLE ROUND, AND ALETA, GREY-EYED QUEEN OF THE MISTY ISLES! THEIR ROMANCE WAS AS A BRIGHT STAR ILLUMINATING THEIR TIMES, BUT NOW THAT LIGHT HAS FLICKERED AND GONE OUT LIKE A SNUFFED CANDLE.'

AND ON THAT DAY ALETA RISES AND GOES ABOUT HER DUTIES CHEERFULLY AS IF THERE WERE NEVER A CARE IN THE WORLD.

ALSO ON THAT DAY PRINCE VALIANT COMES WITHIN SIGHT OF CAMELOT AND HE ALSO IS DOING HIS DUTY BY BEING CHIVALROUS... THE SWEET-SCENTED BUNDLE IN HIS ARMS IS PART OF THAT DUTY.

NO ONE, NOT EVEN VAL, WILL EVER KNOW THE ANXIETY THAT TEARS AT HER HEART AS SHE WATCHES THE ROAD BY WHICH HE WILL RETURN. BUT HIS LOVE OF ADVENTURE, THE PERILOUS QUESTS, HOW OFTEN....? THEN SHE SEES HIM RETURNING AND TEARS OF RELIEF STREAM DOWN HER CHEEKS.

WITH A WILDLY BEATING HEART SHE FLIES TO GREET HIM. HE RIDES INTO THE COURTYARD, GRINNING. THE LADY IN HIS ARMS SEEMS TO BE CLINGING CLOSER THAN SAFETY DEMANDS. "HELLO, ALETA," HE CALLS, "I WOULD LIKE YOU TO MEET THE LADY DONAT."

HE HELPS THE LADY DISMOUNT, BUT WHEN HE TURNS TOWARD THE DOORWAY IT IS EMPTY.

PUZZLED AND ANGRY HE DOES NOT ENTER THE PALACE, BUT RIDES TO HIS HOME IN THE WALLED TOWN BENEATH THE CASTLE BATTLEMENTS.

THE ROOM HE SHARED WITH ALETA IS LOCKED. THERE COMES NO ANSWER TO HIS KNOCK. A SERVANT TELLS HIM: "YOUR THINGS ARE IN THE SPARE BEDROOM UPSTAIRS."

NEXT WEEK— *Parting of the Ways*

Prince Valiant

IN THE DAYS OF KING ARTHUR

BY HAROLD R FOSTER

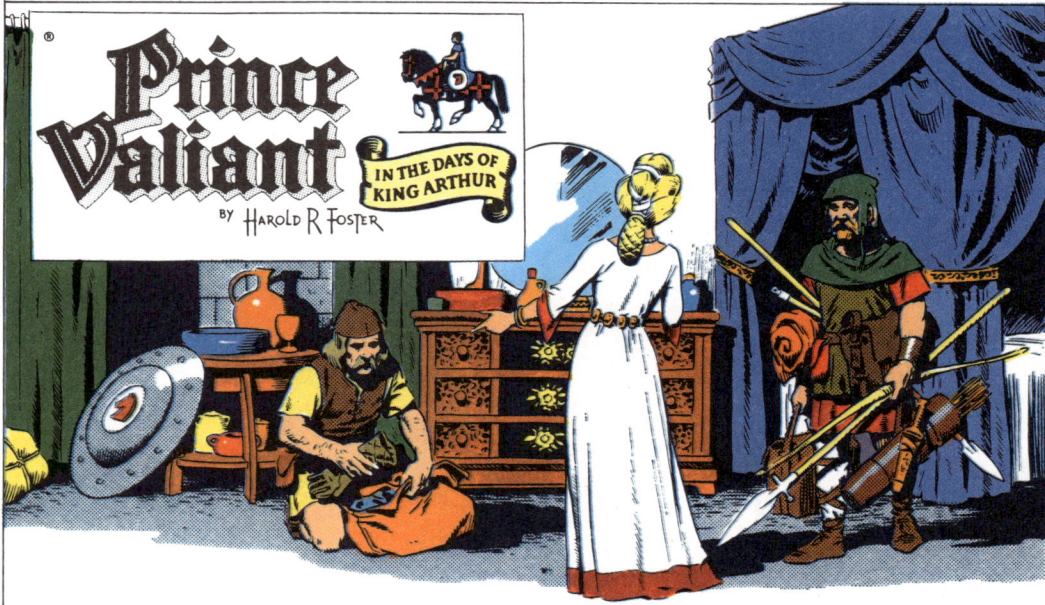

Our Story: NOW THAT SHE HAS BANISHED VAL FOREVER, ALETA CAN AT LAST CLEAN UP THEIR ROOM. HUNTING BOWS, SHEAVES OF ARROWS, HIS OLD BOARSPEAR, THE WORK TABLE WITH ITS ODDS AND ENDS OF ARMOR, MUDDY BOOTS, HUNTING HORN, EVERYTHING.

ALL THE REMINDERS ARE GONE. NOW SHE CAN FORGET HIM. HER HOUSE, UNFORTUNATELY, IS NOW AS NEAT AND BARE AS A CONVENT, NO PLACE FOR SONG AND LAUGHTER.

VAL TAKES UP QUARTERS IN THE CASTLE. "WHAT DID I DO? WHAT MADE HER SO ANGRY? BY THE CINDERS OF HADES, IF SHE THINKS I WILL COME CRAWLING....ETC.....ETC....."

SO VAL PUTS ON A CHEERFUL GRIN AND JOINS THE OTHER KNIGHTS IN THEIR GAMES. SIR GAWAIN IS DELIGHTED TO HAVE HIS BEST FRIEND BACK AND LOOKS FORWARD TO A MERRY EVENING, BUT VAL SOON SINKS INTO SULLEN SILENCE. "WHAT A BORE," GROWLS GAWAIN, "GO TO BED!"

EACH AFTERNOON ALETA APPEARS AT THE PALACE. SHE IS MORE GAY THAN EVER. SHE AND VAL MEET OFTEN AND EXCHANGE POLITE, BUT BRIEF, GREETINGS.

WHAT A VAST AND LONELY DESERT THE BED IS! ONCE UPON A TIME VAL USED TO SPRAWL OVER IT, HOG THE COVERS AND SNORE. GOOD RIDDANCE.

1762 © King Features Syndicate, Inc., 1970. World rights reserved. 11-15

VAL STANDS MOONING BEFORE THE OPEN WINDOW, CATCHES A COLD, AND FOR MANY DAYS WILL HAVE THE SNIFFLES AND A RED NOSE.

NEXT WEEK— The Rift Grows

Prince Valiant

IN THE DAYS OF KING ARTHUR

BY HAROLD R. FOSTER

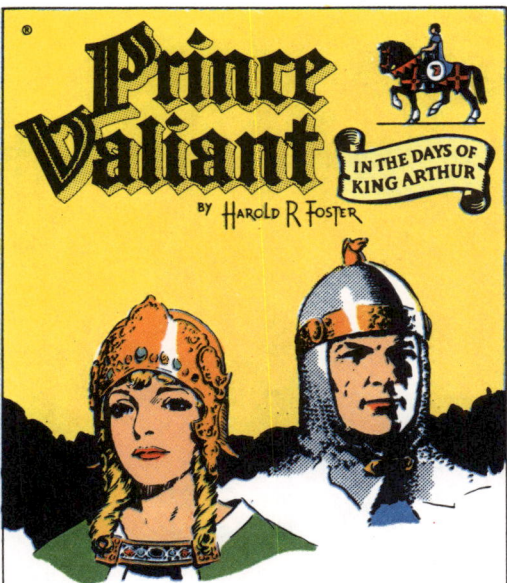

Our Story: ALETA, QUEEN OF THE MISTY ISLES, HAS HER PRIDE, AND PRINCE VALIANT, KNIGHT OF THE ROUND TABLE, HEIR TO THE THRONE OF THULES, ALSO HAS AN UNYIELDING PRIDE. THE CAUSE OF THE RIFT BETWEEN THEM IS FORGOTTEN, ONLY THE PRIDE REMAINS A WALL OF ICE BETWEEN THEM.

VAL ASKS THE KING FOR A MISSION, ANY MISSION, NO MATTER HOW DANGEROUS. THE KING, KNOWING HIS TROUBLES AND NOTING THE DESPERATE, RECKLESS LOOK IN HIS EYES, REFUSES.

"TOO LONG HAVE I LEFT MY KINGDOM IN THE HANDS OF MY MINISTERS AND THE COUNCIL. IN THE SPRING I WILL RETURN AND TAKE MY THRONE AS A GOOD QUEEN SHOULD."

NOW THAT THE CHILDREN WILL TAKE THEIR PLACE IN COURT, STUDY HOURS ARE INCREASED. LATIN, GREEK AND ARABIC MUST BE PERFECT; DEPORTMENT, PROTOCOL AND HISTORY IMPROVED. GALAN REBELS, GRUMBLING: "I DON'T WANT TO BE A PRINCE, IT IS NO FUN!" BUT ALETA SHOWS HIM THE PALM OF HER HAND AND HE RETURNS TO HIS STUDIES.

THE ONLY ACTION VAL CAN FIND IS IN THE ARMORY. BUT IN HIS UNHAPPY FRAME OF MIND HE TRIES TO RELIEVE HIS HURT IN VIOLENCE AND SOON THE OTHER KNIGHTS AVOID PRACTICING WITH HIM.

ALETA HEARS THAT GUNDAR HARL, THE GREAT NAVIGATOR, IS WINTERING IN CAERLEON AND SHE SENDS A MESSAGE: 'PREPARE YOUR SHIP FOR A VOYAGE TO THE MISTY ISLES AS SOON AS WEATHER PERMITS.'

1763   © King Features Syndicate, Inc., 1970. World rights reserved.   11-22

CAUGHT IN A DILEMMA IS ARN: SHOULD HE GO WITH HIS MOTHER OR STAY WITH HIS FATHER? VAL TELLS HIM: "MAKE YOUR OWN DECISION AND STICK TO IT. YOU WOULD NEVER BE HAPPY WITH A DECISION SOMEONE ELSE MADE FOR YOU."

HE PUTS THE SAME QUESTION TO HIS MOTHER AND ALETA SAYS: "YOUR SISTERS AND BROTHER ARE YOUNG AND STILL LOOK TO ME FOR GUIDANCE, BUT YOU ARE ON THE THRESHOLD OF MANHOOD AND MUST CHOOSE YOUR OWN DESTINY."

NEXT WEEK—The Road to Adventure

HAL FOSTER

Prince Valiant

IN THE DAYS OF KING ARTHUR

BY HAROLD R FOSTER

Our Story: ALETA THROWS BACK THE CURTAINS OF HER IMMENSE BUT LONELY BED. THE SUN IS SHINING THROUGH THE PARCHMENT WINDOWPANES AND THE SOUND OF MELTING SNOW DRIPPING FROM THE EAVES HERALDS THE APPROACHING SPRING.

"WHAT A FOOL I AM TO LET A BIT OF JEALOUSY GROW INTO SUCH ABSURD PROPORTIONS! IT IS NOT MY PRIDE SO MUCH AS MY VANITY THAT IS HURT."

HEEDLESS OF THE SLUSH SHE MAKES HER WAY TO THE CASTLE. SHE THINKS OF A HUNDRED ENDEARING THINGS TO SAY TO VAL WHEN ONCE AGAIN SHE IS ENFOLDED IN HIS ARMS.

SHE SEEKS OUT HIS QUARTERS IN THE MERLIN TOWER. IT IS EMPTY. GONE ARE SHIELD AND HELMET, ARMS AND ARMOR AND, MOST SIGNIFICANT OF ALL, HIS SADDLEBAGS. ALETA STANDS SILENT WHILE HER HAPPINESS DRAINS SLOWLY AWAY.

ONCE AGAIN SIR VALIANT RIDES AT ADVENTURE. THERE WILL BE LITTLE CHANCE OF ACTION, FOR NO ONE USES THE ALMOST IMPASSABLE ROADS IN WINTER IF IT CAN BE AVOIDED.

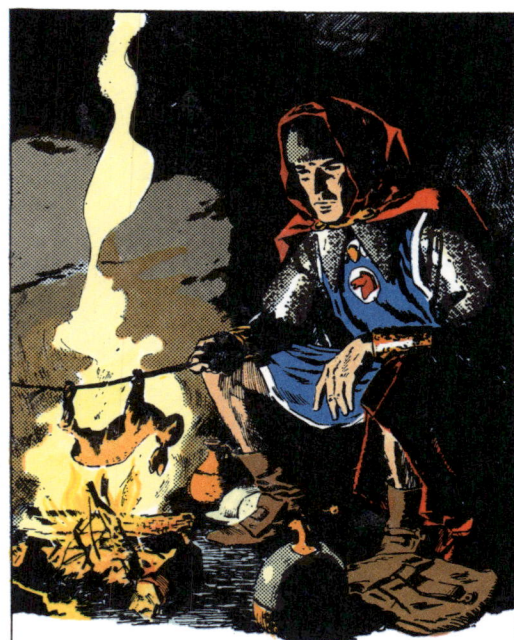

THERE ARE NOT EVEN OUTLAWS TO ENLIVEN HIS WANDERINGS.

THEN COMES A DAY WHEN THINGS BECOME MORE INTERESTING. SIR ASTARIC HAS JUST SETTLED A LABOR DISPUTE WITH HIS SERFS AND IS RETURNING FROM GALLOWS HILL WITH HIS EXECUTIONERS. HE INVITES VAL TO SPEND THE NIGHT IN HIS STRONGHOLD.

NEXT WEEK - The Maiden Fair

1764

11-29

Prince Valiant

IN THE DAYS OF KING ARTHUR

BY HAROLD R. FOSTER

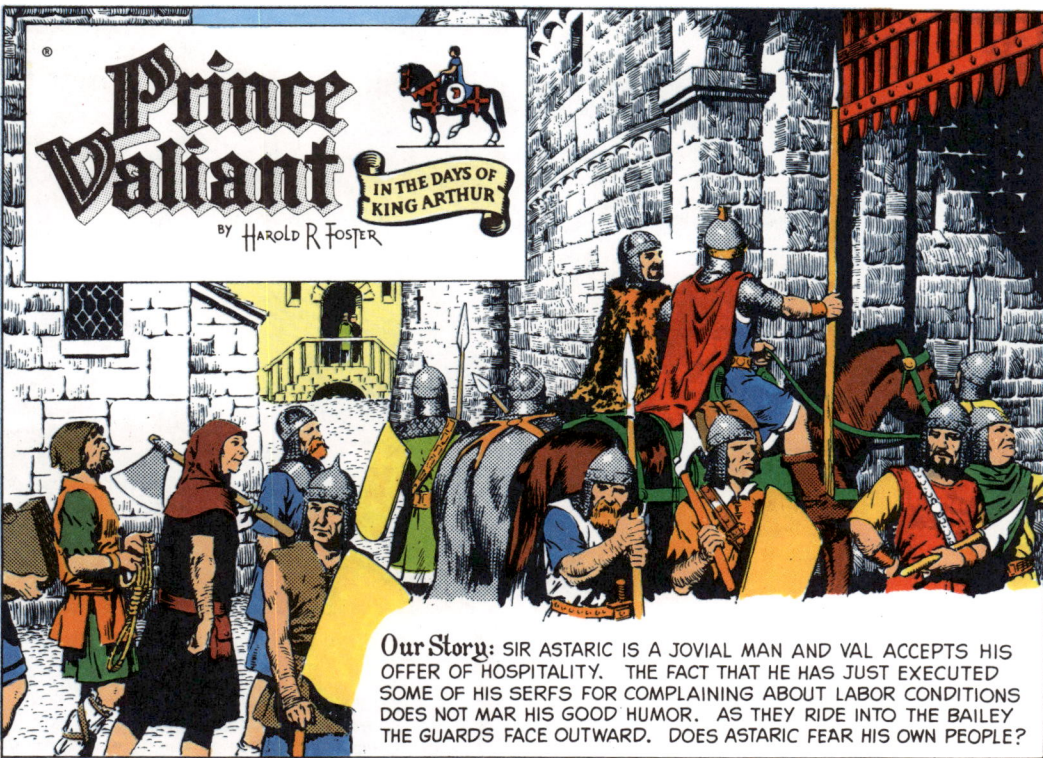

Our Story: SIR ASTARIC IS A JOVIAL MAN AND VAL ACCEPTS HIS OFFER OF HOSPITALITY. THE FACT THAT HE HAS JUST EXECUTED SOME OF HIS SERFS FOR COMPLAINING ABOUT LABOR CONDITIONS DOES NOT MAR HIS GOOD HUMOR. AS THEY RIDE INTO THE BAILEY THE GUARDS FACE OUTWARD. DOES ASTARIC FEAR HIS OWN PEOPLE?

THE ENTRANCE TO THE KEEP IS LOW, THE THRESHOLD HIGH, MAKING IT IMPOSSIBLE FOR A VISITOR TO DEFEND HIMSELF SHOULD HE BE UNWELCOME.

ASTARIC'S CHAIR TOUCHES THE WALL SO NO ONE CAN GET BEHIND HIM, HIS WEAPONS AT HAND. THIS WAS THE CUSTOM IN THE OLD DAYS WHEN WAR AND RAIDS WERE COMMON. VAL'S HOST SEEMS TO THINK THESE ARRANGEMENTS ARE STILL NECESSARY.

HE ASSURES VAL THAT HE IS A TRUE SUPPORTER OF ARTHUR, AND BRAGS OF VALIANT DEEDS DONE IN THE KING'S BEHALF. HE IS ANXIOUS TO KNOW IF THE KING WOULD GO TO HIS ASSISTANCE IF HE WERE ATTACKED BY HIS VILE NEIGHBORS.

BEFORE RETIRING, VAL, AS USUAL, GOES TO THE STABLES TO MAKE SURE ARVAK IS WELL CARED FOR. ON HIS RETURN AN OLD ROMANTIC STORY IS BEING ENACTED...

....A FAIR MAIDEN WITH GOLDEN TRESSES PLEADS TO BE RESCUED FROM A GRIM TOWER IN WHICH SHE IS IMPRISONED. A NOTE FLUTTERS DOWN. HOW FAMILIAR THIS ALL IS!

HE HAS HEARD TROUBADOURS RECITE THIS OLD ROMANTIC TALE MANY TIMES. HE SHOULD TRY TO RESCUE HER WHILE EVERYONE HAS A GOOD LAUGH? WITH A CYNICAL GRIN HE TUCKS THE NOTE IN HIS TUNIC.

NEXT WEEK — *Encore*

1765   © King Features Syndicate, Inc., 1970. World rights reserved.   12-6

Prince Valiant

IN THE DAYS OF KING ARTHUR

BY HAROLD R FOSTER

Our Story: HOW OFTEN HAD PRINCE VALIANT HEARD THE ROMANTIC TALE OF THE FAIR MAID WITH GOLDEN HAIR, LOCKED IN A GRIM TOWER AND PLEADING FOR A GALLANT KNIGHT ERRANT TO RESCUE HER? WITH A WRY SMILE HE TUCKS HER NOTE IN HIS TUNIC.

"I WOULD WAGER THAT SIR ASTARIC AND HIS FRIENDS ARE WAITING FOR ME TO SALLY FORTH TO THE RESCUE WHILE THEY HAVE A GOOD LAUGH." THEN HE REMEMBERS THE NOTE.

"TO THE EARL OF BURNFORD: FATHER, I HAVE FALLEN INTO THE HANDS OF SIR ASTARIC, TO BE FORCED TO WED HIS HORRIBLE SON. TELL GUIVERIC I LOVE HIM, BUT IN HEAVEN'S NAME COME QUICKLY."

THE MESSAGE HAS A GENUINE APPEAL, SO WHEN VAL ENTERS THE DINING HALL HE IS ALERT. THE ENTRANCE IS SMALL AND LOW, ONE MAN COULD DEFEND IT AGAINST MANY. THE HOUSE CARLS ARE FULLY ARMED BUT THE SOLDIERS LEAVE ALL WEAPONS OUTSIDE. WHY?

SIR ASTARIC COMES OUT TO THE COURTYARD TO BID VAL A GOOD-BYE. A HEAVY WATER PITCHER MISSES HIM BY INCHES AND SHATTERS AT HIS FEET. ALL EYES TURN UPWARD WHERE THE FAIR MAID WITH GOLDEN HAIR IS TAKING AIM WITH THE BASIN.

"YOU EVIL TOAD!" SHE SCREAMS, "SET ME FREE OR MY FATHER WILL DESTROY YOU AND YOUR STINKING NEST!" "PAY NO ATTENTION," ADVISES ASTARIC. "SHE IS JUST BEING LOCKED IN HER ROOM UNTIL SHE LEARNS POLITENESS."

PRINCE VALIANT CAN SEE NO WAY IN WHICH HE, SINGLE-HANDED, CAN RESCUE THE MAID IN THE TOWER, SO HE CALMLY RIDES AWAY. HOWEVER, HIS EYES TAKE IN EVERY DETAIL OF THE DEFENSES, FOR HE WILL RETURN.

THE BURNED HOMESTEADS AND WEED-GROWN FIELDS INDICATE THAT CONSTANT WARS TROUBLE THIS LAND. TOWARD SUNSET HE IS CHALLENGED BY A LONE KNIGHT.

NEXT WEEK— *The Hothead*

1766   © King Features Syndicate, Inc., 1970. World rights reserved.   12-13

1766

Prince Valiant
IN THE DAYS OF KING ARTHUR
BY HAROLD R FOSTER

Our Story: BY THE EAGER WAY HE DRESSES HIS SHIELD AND LOWERS HIS LANCE, PRINCE VALIANT JUDGES THE STRANGER TO BE VERY YOUNG.
"STAND AND STATE YOUR BUSINESS," HE DEMANDS. "IT IS NONE OF YOURS," ANSWERS VAL CALMLY.

"RUDELY SAID," SPUTTERS THE YOUTH, "AND BY MY SHIELD AND LANCE I WILL CORRECT YOUR MANNERS!"
"I HAVE MORE IMPORTANT MATTERS THAN INTRODUCING YOU TO THE TURF. CAN YOU LEAD ME TO EARL BURNFORD?"

"YES, BUT NOT NOW, FOR I SEEK HIS DAUGHTER, MY BETROTHED! HAVE YOU SEEN HER IN YOUR WANDERINGS? YOU WOULD KNOW HER BY HER WONDROUS BEAUTY, HER GOLDEN HAIR."
"YES, I HAVE SEEN HER," ANSWERS VAL. "SHE IS A PRISONER IN SIR ASTARIC'S CASTLE."

"THEN I GO TO RESCUE HER. I'LL BEARD THE SNEAKY ASTARIC IN HIS DEN! I'LL......." VAL LOWERS HIS LANCE POINT, BARRING THE WAY. "ENOUGH! STOP THINKING OF YOURSELF AS THE BRAVE YOUNG HERO OF A BALLAD. THE GIRL IS IN DANGER. NOW LEAD ME TO BURNFORD, AND WE WILL PLAN A REAL RESCUE."

YOUNG GUIVERIC CURBS HIS IMPATIENCE AND LEADS THE WAY TO BURNFORD. THE EARL RECEIVES THE NEWS WITH MIXED EMOTIONS; DELIGHTED THAT HIS DAUGHTER HAS BEEN FOUND, BUT FEARFUL OF HER FATE IN ASTARIC'S HANDS.

VAL LETS HIM READ THE NOTE HIS DAUGHTER HAD WRITTEN. "SO! ASTARIC WOULD FORCE MY DAUGHTER TO WED HIS HALF-WIT SON. WHAT A GHASTLY SITUATION. LET US MAKE PLANS AT ONCE!"

DAWN COMES ERE PLANS ARE COMPLETE. ASTARIC HAS EVERY ADVANTAGE—MORE MEN, STRONG WALLS, AN IMPREGNABLE KEEP. STRATEGY IS ALL-IMPORTANT, AND VAL PLANS A STRANGE CAMPAIGN.

1767

NEXT WEEK— **The War of the Stomach** 12-20

Prince Valiant
IN THE DAYS OF KING ARTHUR
BY HAROLD R. FOSTER

Our Story: DAWN, AND THE GATES OF BURNFORD CASTLE SWING WIDE AND MESSENGERS RIDE FORTH TO SUMMON THE CLAN LEADERS TO HELP IN THE RESCUE OF THE EARL'S DAUGHTER FROM THE SOILED HANDS OF SIR ASTARIC.

YOUNG GUIVERIC, THE HOTHEAD, EXCLAIMS, "WHY ALL THIS DELAY WHEN MY BETROTHED LANGUISHES IN HER PRISON? BATTER DOWN THE GATES AND I WILL HEW A PATH TO HER WITH MY SWORD!"
"I WILL SHOW YOU WHY," ANSWERS VAL. "COME WITH ME TO THE GYMNASIUM."

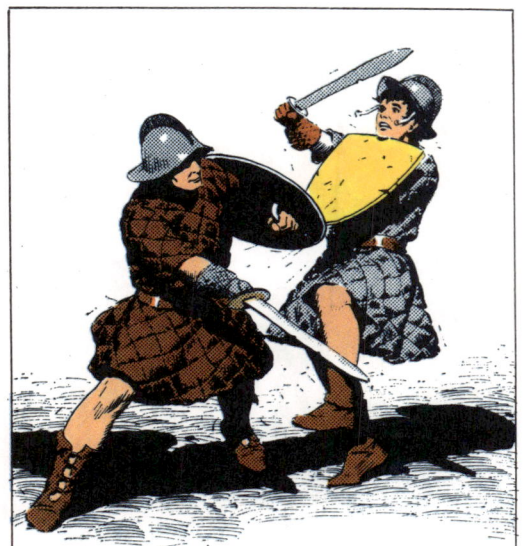

VAL GIVES THE UNSKILLED YOUTH A THOROUGH THRASHING. "YOU WILL NEED YEARS OF PRACTICE BEFORE YOU CAN LIVE UP TO YOUR HEROIC WORDS," SAYS VAL. "WITH COURAGE YOU CAN FACE DANGER, BUT ONLY BY SKILL CAN YOU SURVIVE IT."

ONCE MORE SIR ASTARIC DEMANDS THAT HIS PRISONER WED HIS SON. SHE IS SHACKLED, FOR THIS MAID WITH THE GOLDEN HAIR IS NOT EXACTLY AMIABLE AND HER ANSWER IS ENOUGH TO CURL HIS BEARD. "TAKE HER AWAY," HE GROWLS. "SHE WILL SULK IN HER ROOM UNTIL SHE CURBS HER TEMPER!"

FIRST TO SET OUT IS PRINCE VALIANT. NO CATAPULTS OR BATTERING-RAMS DOES HE TAKE, ONLY PACK HORSES LOADED WITH FOOD. SPRING IS THE SEASON OF STARVATION WITH THE WINTER'S SUPPLY OF FOOD EXHAUSTED AND PLANTING NOT YET BEGUN. VAL HAS FIGURED THAT HE CAN BETTER OPEN THE CASTLE GATES WITH A LOAF OF BREAD THAN A RAM.

TO AVOID BEING SEEN FROM THE BATTLEMENTS HE ENTERS THE VILLAGE AT EVENTIDE. AT SIGHT OF MOUNTED MEN ALL DOORS SLAM SHUT AND BOLTS ARE SHOT HOME. IN THE SILENCE THAT FOLLOWS VAL SHOUTS, "I HAVE BREAD!"

1768   © King Features Syndicate, Inc. 1970. World rights reserved.   12-27

HUNGER OVERCOMES FEAR AND SOON THE SERFS ARE CLAMORING FOR THIS HEAVEN-SENT BOUNTY. "THERE WILL BE WAR," VAL TELLS THEM, "BUT YOU, YOUR HOMES AND CATTLE WILL NOT BE TOUCHED. WE WAR ON ASTARIC ONLY."

THE WATCHMEN ON THE GATE THAT GUARDS THE BRIDGE LOOK AT EACH OTHER IN ASTONISHMENT. FOR THE FIRST TIME THEY CAN REMEMBER LIGHTS APPEAR IN THE VILLAGE AND THERE ARE SOUNDS OF LAUGHTER!

NEXT WEEK - A Strange War

Prince Valiant
IN THE DAYS OF KING ARTHUR
BY HAROLD R FOSTER

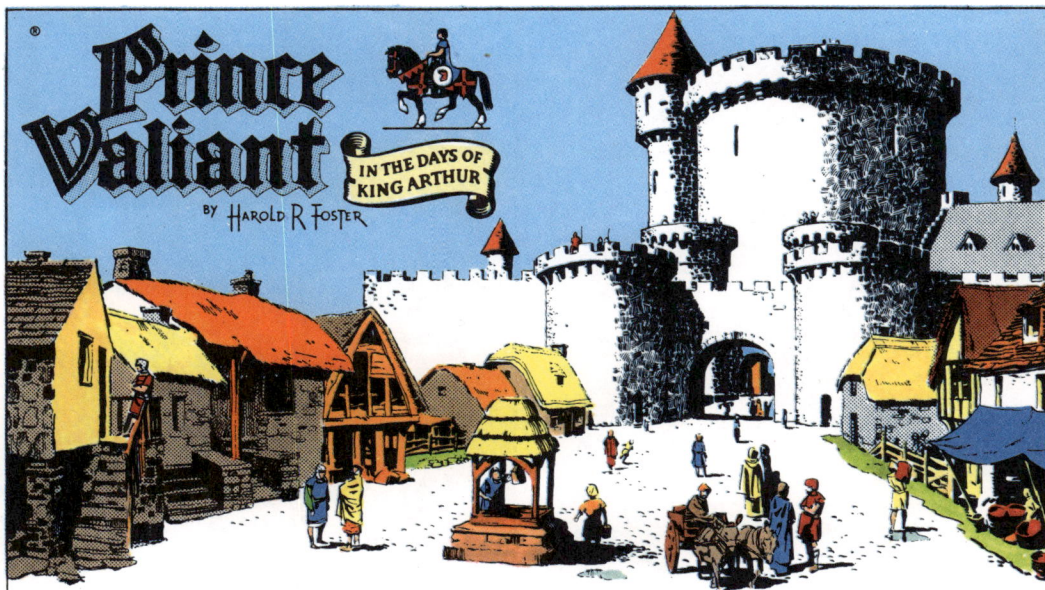

Our Story: PRINCE VALIANT REHEARSES IN HIS MIND THE FACTS HE KNOWS OF SIR ASTARIC'S STRONGHOLD: FIRST, THE VILLAGE WHERE THE ENSLAVED SERFS ARE OVERWORKED, OVERTAXED AND UNDERFED. THEN THE BATTLEMENTS, MANNED BY ARCHERS, MOST OF WHOM HAVE FAMILIES IN THE VILLAGE. NEXT, THE KEEP WHERE ASTARIC, SURROUNDED BY HARDY HOUSE CARLS, LIVES IN SECURITY.

IT IS THE CUSTOM OF THE GUARDS AT THE BRIDGE GATE TO SLIP OUT AT NIGHT AND CARRY PACKAGES OF FOOD, SAVED FROM THEIR MEAGER RATIONS, TO THEIR PEOPLE IN THE VILLAGE.

BY THIS MEANS THE GOSSIP OF THE VILLAGE SPREADS THROUGH THE GARRISON, AS VAL INTENDED: WAR IS COMING, THE SERFS WILL NOT BE KILLED, THEIR HOMES BURNED AND THE CATTLE DRIVEN OFF, AS WAS THE CUSTOM IN THOSE DAYS. THE ENEMY IS, IN FACT, FEEDING THE VILLAGERS.

THE EARL OF BURNFORD ARRIVES AFTER A LONG STRUGGLE TO BRING PROVISIONS AND WAR MACHINES THROUGH THE MUD OF THE ALMOST IMPASSABLE ROADS. AND ASTARIC AWAKES WITH AN OATH: *"WHAT FOOL WOULD START A WAR AT THIS TIME OF YEAR?"*

IN A TOWER WINDOW THERE IS A FLASH OF GOLD. THE EARL'S DAUGHTER SEES HER FATHER'S ARRIVAL. *"IT IS ABOUT TIME SOMEONE CAME TO RESCUE ME FROM THIS CHILLY PRISON,"* SHE SNAPS.

"PATIENCE, MY LOVE, FOR BY MY SWORD AND SHIELD I SWEAR TO FIGHT UNTIL DEATH IN YOUR SERVICE!" CRIES GUIVERIC. *"DO YOU MIND IF WE HELP A LITTLE BIT?"* ASKS VAL SARCASTICALLY.

1769   © King Features Syndicate, Inc., 1970. World rights reserved.   1-3

PRINCE VALIANT STANDS BEFORE THE BRIDGE GATE AND CALLS FOR A MEETING WITH ITS CAPTAIN, AND WITH HIM ARE THAT CAPTAIN'S WIFE AND SON.

NEXT WEEK — A Simple Question

1769

Prince Valiant
IN THE DAYS OF KING ARTHUR
BY Harold R. Foster

Our Story: PRINCE VALIANT SEEKS A MEETING WITH THE CAPTAIN OF THE BRIDGE GATE. TO GUARD AGAINST TREACHERY HE TAKES ALONG THE CAPTAIN'S WIFE AND SON. HE HAS ALREADY WON THE FAVOR OF THE GARRISON BY SAVING THE VILLAGERS FROM HUNGER. THIS IS WHAT HE TELLS:

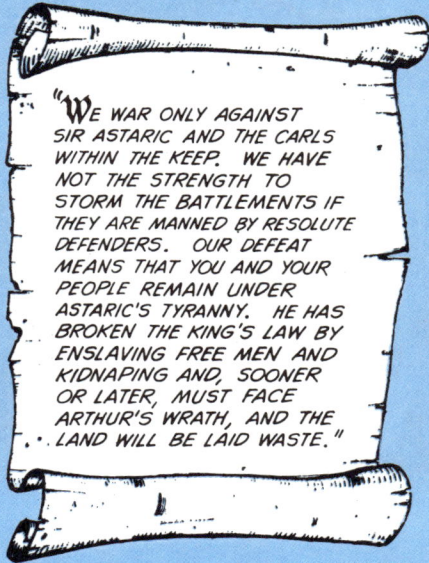

"WE WAR ONLY AGAINST SIR ASTARIC AND THE CARLS WITHIN THE KEEP. WE HAVE NOT THE STRENGTH TO STORM THE BATTLEMENTS IF THEY ARE MANNED BY RESOLUTE DEFENDERS. OUR DEFEAT MEANS THAT YOU AND YOUR PEOPLE REMAIN UNDER ASTARIC'S TYRANNY. HE HAS BROKEN THE KING'S LAW BY ENSLAVING FREE MEN AND KIDNAPING AND, SOONER OR LATER, MUST FACE ARTHUR'S WRATH, AND THE LAND WILL BE LAID WASTE."

SIR ASTARIC'S BATTLE PLANS ARE SIMPLE. HE TELLS HIS CARLS: "OUR ARCHERS WILL PICK OFF THE ENEMY AS THEY CROSS THE BRIDGE. THE SOLDIERS WILL DEFEND THE BATTLEMENTS TO THE END. ONLY IF THE WALL IS BREACHED AND THE KEEP THREATENED, NEED WE FIGHT."

THE BATTLE BEGINS AT THE BRIDGE GATE AMID A HAIL OF ARROWS. MIRACULOUSLY, NO ONE IS HIT AND THE GATES YIELD TO THE FIRST BLOW OF THE RAM.

EARL BURNFORD LEADS THE WAY ACROSS THE BRIDGE, NOTING, WITH A GRIN, THAT THERE IS NO SIGN OF BLOOD ANYWHERE AND THE DEAD AND WOUNDED ALL SEEM TO HAVE FALLEN IN COMFORTABLE POSITIONS.

THE ARCHERS ON THE MAIN GATE AND CURTAIN WALL SEEM TO AIM CAREFULLY AT OPEN SPACES; THEN, SUDDENLY MEN BEGIN TO FALL. GLANCING UP FROM UNDER HIS SHIELD VAL SEES SOMETHING HE HAD NOT FORESEEN....

....FROM THE PARAPET OF THE KEEP THE CARLS SEND DOWN A SLEET STORM OF ARROWS AND THEY HAVE COMMAND OF THE BRIDGE, THE WALL AND THE COURTYARD.

THE MAIN GATE OPENS TO THE INVADERS AND THEY FIND SHELTER FROM THE ARROWS IN THE BARRACKS. "FOUL TRAITORS!" ROARS ASTARIC, "WE ARE BETRAYED. SHOOT ANYONE YOU SEE BELOW!"

NEXT WEEK— The Breakthrough

1770   © King Features Syndicate, Inc., 1971. World rights reserved.   1-10

Prince Valiant
IN THE DAYS OF KING ARTHUR
BY HAROLD R FOSTER

Our Story: BY STRATEGY THE OUTER WALL HAS BEEN TAKEN, AND WITHIN THE SHELTER OF THE GATEWAY EARL BURNFORD AND PRINCE VALIANT LOOK ACROSS THE COURTYARD TO THE ENTRANCE OF THE KEEP. ARCHERS AND ROCK THROWERS FROM THE PARAPET ABOVE MAKE THIS A DEATH TRAP.

ANYONE WHO SURVIVES THE CROSSING WILL FIND THE SMALL ENTRANCE EASILY DEFENDED. FOR VAL HAD ENTERED ONCE AND REMEMBERS HOW DEFENSELESS HE HAD BEEN.

BUT ENTER THEY MUST, FOR THERE ARE NOT ENOUGH PROVISIONS FOR A SIEGE. LONELY AND UNHAPPY SINCE HE AND ALETA PARTED, IT IS NATURAL FOR HIM TO ADOPT A DESPERATE PLAN.

THE GREAT IRON-STUDDED GATES ARE SET ON THE CARRIAGE OF A DISMANTLED CATAPULT AND TRUNDLED TO THE ENTRANCE AMID A SHOWER OF MISSILES. VAL AND THE VOLUNTEERS LINE UP, CROUCHING LIKE SPRINTERS.

VAL COMES THROUGH LIKE A HURLED SPEAR!

EVEN AS HE LEAPS TO HIS FEET THE 'SINGING SWORD' IS EXULTING AS IT GOES ABOUT ITS LETHAL WORK.

THE SMALL SPACE HE HAS CLEARED AT THE DOORWAY WIDENS AS MORE WARRIORS RUSH THROUGH. ASTARIC SEES HIS CARLS CROWDED BACK AMONG THE TABLES AND BENCHES: "CALL THE ARCHERS DOWN," HE ORDERS. "MEN! TO THE STAIRWAY! CONFINE THE ENEMY TO THE MAIN HALL!"

NEXT WEEK – The Battle for the Stairway

1771   © King Features Syndicate, Inc., 1971. World rights reserved.   1-17

1771

Prince Valiant
IN THE DAYS OF KING ARTHUR
BY HAROLD R. FOSTER

Our Story: PRINCE VALIANT'S NIMBLE SWORD CLEARED THE WAY FOR THOSE WHO FOLLOWED CLOSE BEHIND. SIR ASTARIC IS TAKEN BY SURPRISE. "TO THE STAIRWAY," HE BELLOWS.

NOW ASTARIC AND HIS CARLS HAVE THE ADVANTAGE AS MORE OF HIS MEN LEAVE THE BATTLEMENTS AND JOIN THE FIGHT. "THE ARCHERS! CALL DOWN THE ARCHERS FROM THE TOWERS," HE COMMANDS.

THE ARCHERS SWARM ONTO THE MUSICIANS' BALCONY AND BEGIN TO PICK OFF BURNFORD'S MEN. "TAKE SHELTER UNDER THE TABLES," VAL ORDERS, FOR A PLAN IS TAKING FORM. WORD IS PASSED ALONG AND THE TABLES FORM A LINE.

"CHARGE!" AND THE HEAVY OAKEN TABLES BECOME ONE LONG BATTERING RAM. PROPELLED BY HALF A HUNDRED WARRIORS IT CRASHES AGAINST THE PILLAR SUPPORTING THE GALLERY. AMID THE WRECKAGE THE FIGHT ENDS.

GUIVERIC HAD BELIEVED THAT A HERO COULD ALWAYS HEW HIS WAY TO VICTORY, AS THE TROUBADOURS USED TO SING. BUT THE FIRST GRINNING VETERAN HE MEETS LAYS HIM LOW. PERHAPS HE IS NOT A HERO.

THE CAUSE OF ALL THIS UNREST IS RELEASED. "WHAT KEPT YOU SO LONG, FATHER?" SHE COMPLAINS. THEN FLINGING HERSELF INTO EARL BURNFORD'S ARMS SHE BURSTS INTO TEARS OF RELIEF. "AND GUIVERIC, IS HE SAFE?" SHE INQUIRES.

VICTORY! THE CASTLE HAS BEEN WON, THE FAIR MAID RESCUED, AND GUIVERIC HAS SURVIVED HIS FIRST BATTLE. VAL SHEATHES THE 'SINGING SWORD'. SOMEHOW THERE IS NO FEELING OF DANGER FACED, ODDS OVERCOME... JUST WEARINESS

NEXT WEEK - The Passing Ship

"NOW! HOW IN HEAVEN'S NAME DID YOU ESCAPE FROM THAT DUNGEON?" WONDERS VAL. "YOU ARRIVED JUST IN TIME, FOR I WAS RUNNING OUT OF MAGIC TRICKS."

VAL STANDS MOONING BEFORE THE OPEN WINDOW, CATCHES A COLD, AND FOR MANY DAYS WILL HAVE THE SNIFFLES AND A RED NOSE.

NEXT WEEK– The Rift Grows

EDITOR'S NOTE:

Beginning with this volume, the art duties on *Prince Valiant* began their transfer to the capable hands of John Cullen Murphy. Mr. Murphy, in fact, illustrated six pages in this edition: 1760, 1764, 1766, 1769, 1771, and 1772.

However, there are also a couple of pinch-hitting surprises in store for *Valiant* fans in this volume. Page 1757 was illustrated by veteran cartoonist Gray Morrow (top), and the sharp-eyed reader will probably recognize page 1762 (above) as the handiwork of the legendary EC and MAD artist Wallace Wood. Moreover, *Prince Valiant* expert Rick Norwood —the proprietor of Manuscript Press, publishers of a super-deluxe edition of early *Prince Valiant* episodes (send for information: P.O. Box 336, Moutain Home, TN 37684)— claims that pages 1765, 1767, and 1770 are in fact neither by Foster nor by any of the above gentlemen, but by hands unknown.